The Killing at Circle C

When Daniel Sagger flees from his home, leaving his wife with her throat cut, his son Will can reach but one conclusion: his father is a callous murderer. But this is a crime so horrific it beggars belief, and when Will rides into town to talk to his friends, he discovers an ever-thickening web of intrigue.

Why have men from Hole In The Wall been talking to his father? Who is the mysterious Amos Skillin who has been plying his father with drink? What part do Beebob Hawkins and Texas Dean play in the mystery?

Knowing that he must ride to Hole In The Wall to discover what lies buried in his father's past, Will Sagger heads out with gunsmith Jake Cree and Deputy Slim Gillo. They are destined to ride through hell and to face desperate outlaws in a blazing, bloody climax.

The Killing at Circle C

JACK SHERIFF

A Black Horse Western

ROBERT HALE · LONDON

ISBN 0 7090 7493 X

Robert Hale Limited
Clerkenwell House
Clerkenwell Green
London EC1R 0HT

Typeset by
Derek Doyle & Associates, Liverpool.
Printed and bound in Great Britain by
Antony Rowe Limited, Wiltshire

Dedicated to Christopher Hurst,
grandson number one,
always a country boy.

CHAPTER ONE

How do you talk sense into your pa when he's gone missing after killing your ma, slicing her throat open in the cold wet hours before dawn when he'd ridden home from town with a bellyful of harsh whiskey and a mind addled by weeks of worry?

How do you explain to a younger sister that the bloody sight that met her terrified gaze when she walked through from her bedroom – disturbed by the fading rattle of hooves, nostrils twitching at the raw, coppery smell – would fade with time, the nightmares that would so many times bring her bolt-upright in her bed cease, the hatred for a grey-haired man wither and be replaced by warmer memories?

'And why,' Will Sagger whispered, 'would I waste my time doing any of that if the ageing man some-where out there with what's left of his dignity is running away from a crime he didn't commit, each haunted night since then spent staring up at a necklace of stars and visualizing a dangling noose ready to be jerked tight around his corded throat if ever he's caught?'

Why?

Who had done this?

Those last questions were thought, not spoken, for halfway between home and town at this hour there was nobody to give an answer. Last night's moon was a fading crescent in pale-blue skies. Under the trees the air was already richly scented as the fast-rising sun warmed grey-green leaves bright with the freshness of early spring, the silence as yet unbroken by the hum of insects. The more pungent aroma of Sagger's cigarette cut sharply into that still, fresh air and, with a gesture taut with contained anger, he flicked it away. Beneath him, his bay horse moved restlessly, one ear flicking and, with a distant smile, Sagger touched it lightly with his heels and moved across the coarse grass and out on to the trail.

As he rode towards town, carrying with him the news that he had tried hard to keep within the confines of Bar C until grief faded and there was a return to sanity, Will Sagger struggled to come to terms with tragedy. But, most of all, he tried to figure out if the one glaring anomaly in Daniel Sagger's hurried departure carried some hidden meaning, or was the oversight of a man hit by panic; to decide if his pa had broken the habit that had been with him since the 1870s – more than a decade – out of desperation or in a silent scream for help?

Two days had passed since the killing, and to the outside world Bar C, the small cattle ranch the stricken Daniel Sagger had ridden away from, remained unchanged. Day-to-day work had continued as usual under the guidance of long-time foreman, Dave Lee Nelson; spring roundup was still some weeks away, and the three hands retained over the winter months were not yet overworked with chores.

At dawn on the first day, Mary Ann Sagger had been buried in the small plot behind the ranch house. It was then that Will had gone into the bunkhouse with the three 'punchers and asked them to stay around the ranch; to keep the news of what had happened under their hats. As far as he knew, the men had complied. Wages weren't due for a couple of weeks, and he'd guessed shrewdly that all three were still bust from their last month-end spree.

Another day had dragged by, and he had kept that for Becky. Ten years old, tow-headed and pigtailed, she had become a little girl in a calico frock who wandered aimlessly about the yard in bright sunlight looking at the world through wide blue eyes that saw only horror. In time, that would change. Will Sagger gave himself to her for that day, gave her the comfort of an older brother's embrace when it was needed, at night sat with her in the warm lamplight while she tossed and turned her way into an uneasy sleep haunted by terrible dreams.

He had done what he could for what was left of

his family, yet still he continued along the lonely trail south with trepidation. Bar C was an hour's ride north of the town of Ten Mile Halt, which was located on Beaver Creek some way south of Sundance. He'd deliberately stopped halfway to rest and gather his thoughts, but all he'd achieved was to create more turmoil in a mind worn out with too much thinking. And with the town shimmering some way ahead but too close for comfort in his present state, he was still mentally juggling words. Quite soon he would be talking to gunsmith Jake Cree, a long-time friend; to Red Keegan, who had stood like a rock behind the bar in his saloon and tried to curb Daniel Sagger's drinking; to Marshal Cliff McLure, who would perhaps look with suspicion at the time elapsed between killing and Sagger's ride to town – and he had no idea what he was going to say.

So it must be Jake Cree first. The easy way out. Troubles told first to a willing listener who would weigh them with wisdom, balance truth against lies, the possible against the improbable. And it was down the south side of Ten Mile Halt's main street that Will Sagger rode, to tie the blood bay at the rail still deep in shadow and push his way through the familiar door with its jingling bell into a room smelling of metal and gun oil where a man with sharp blue eyes waited behind a stained counter.

'Jake,' Will Sagger said – then his throat locked, and he braced his arms on the oily timber top and after two days the tears came and Jake Cree came fast around the counter and in a room seemingly walled with rifles and other weapons of death a tall man rested his head on a shorter man's broad shoulder and wept without shame.

CHAPTER TWO

In the back room they sipped hot, strong coffee. Jake was perched on a work bench, muscular and aproned, ready for a day's work but his bearded face lined with deep concern. Will Sagger sat on a stool, hunched with the effort of holding back his grief. He had told his story, seen the shock hit Cree, watched that shock fade and the wheels begin turning in the mind of the man who had been Daniel Sagger's friend for more than twenty years.

Now Cree said flatly, 'Daniel wouldn't kill Mary Ann.'

'Not unless he was crazy.'

'And was he? I took a drink with him a week ago. He was worried, but wouldn't say why. Had he slipped further?'

'Not noticeably. But it seems he rode to town that night, came back so late everyone was asleep. . . .' Sagger shrugged, bent to his coffee.

'What was getting to him, Will? What was turning a good man into a drunk?'

'I asked him several times. He wouldn't say.'

Sagger looked up. 'So maybe we need to look further back, at times before he had a family; maybe we need to look at the younger Daniel Sagger.'

'Before my time.'

'Christ, Jake, he must have talked, reminisced.'

'We all do. But what truth is there in that kind of talk? When a man's looking down his back-trail, how do you sift hard facts from tall tales?'

'With hindsight. Or is it foresight? I don't know. But maybe something he said about the past will make more sense in the light of what he's done.'

'And what has he done? Gone missing for two days—'

'Rode out fast with his wife still bleeding her life away—'

'Or been taken.'

Sudden silence.

'How many horses did you hear?'

'None. Becky woke first. Went through. Found . . .'

Words failed him.

'Where were *you*, Will?'

'Sleeping.'

'There's some who'll find that hard to believe, you a few feet away in the next room. A man rides home to Bar C full of liquor, clatters into the yard. Then a woman's murdered. You mean to tell me there was no argument? Did he just walk in and slit her throat?

'Pa didn't kill her!'

'Someone did. But unless he was Banquo's ghost he'd have anounced his presence. And he did. He woke Becky.'

'The hands heard nothing.'

'They were used to Daniel riding in late. One more time would have no more impact on their dreams than a warm spring breeze. Besides, they were across the yard in the bunkhouse.'

'Jake,' Will Sagger said, 'what the hell are you suggesting?'

Cree shook his head. 'Not a damn thing. What I'm doing is preparing you for what you're going to face when you talk to Ciff McLure.'

Sagger rose from the stool, put the cup on the work bench, looked through the uncurtained rear window and across the scattering of tar-paper shacks on the outskirts of Ten Mile Halt. He'd told Jake Cree the truth, but with badge-toting Cliff McLure that might not be such a good idea. Why risk complications that could lead to trouble? Mary Ann Sagger had been laid to rest. If he told McLure pneumonia took her to her grave, there would be compassion, not suspicion. And Jake Cree would keep his mouth shut.

'Why would Pa be taken, Jake?'

'I shouldn't have said that.'

Sagger swung to face the gunsmith, met the clear blue eyes, saw the barriers come down.

'But you did. And you suggested what Becky heard was more than one horse. So who are we talking about?'

'Go talk to McLure.'

'With the truth?' Sagger's laugh was brittle. 'Hell, what is the truth?'

'McLure is the law, he's got sharp ears and a

deputy with a long nose. Also, your pa's been spending a lot of time with his elbow on Red Keegan's bar. So when you're finished with McLure and Slim Gillo, we'll cross the street and I'll buy you a drink.' Cree drained his coffee, his eyes suddenly clear and knowing. 'I can't see you letting this lie, Will. You're going after your pa. When you do you'll need all the information you can get.'

Cliff McLure was a long beanpole with a lean waist and hips sharp enough to cut through his sagging leather gunbelt. His roll-top desk, safe, window ledges and almost everything else in the room at the front of the jail were filmed with dust. Even his thatch of coarse hair looked as if it had been dusted with grey, but the rack of guns against the back wall glistened with an oily sheen, the notice board with Wanted dodgers, election notices, railroad timetables and scrawled reminders was well kept, and the marshal's deep-set, tawny eyes were as bright as brass buttons.

'You're no stranger to me, Will, but this wild story you've rode in with knocks me back a couple of steps, leaves me winded. Your ma dead and buried after a knifing, you say – and your pa gone?'

'Two days ago.'

McLure hitched his pants, and pulled at his lean jaw.

'And your reading of this . . . situation?'

'Nobody broke into the house. Everything points to Pa cutting Ma's throat, getting back on his horse and hightailing. I don't believe that.'

'No, I'd be mighty hard pressed to think that of your pa. But you say getting *back* on his horse? Does that mean he'd just got off it?'

'He'd been into town, rode home in the rain full of drink and—'

'You saw him?'

'No, I was asleep.'

For a moment McLure looked at Sagger in silence, lips pursed. Then he gestured him to a seat and said, 'Will, tell me what you know, not what you surmise.'

Will Sagger sighed. 'I woke up when Becky started screaming. I went through. She was in the middle of the living-room, looking down at Ma.' He shrugged helplessly. 'She was flat on her back, covered in blood . . .'

'What time did your pa go out?'

'Early afternoon.'

'And that's the last you saw of him?'

Sagger nodded.

'So, your ma stayed up late—'

'With me, waiting for him.'

'—Becky was in bed, then you started yawning and your ma told you she'd wait on her own and you went to your room and the next thing you know your sister's screaming?'

'Right.'

McLure folded his rawboned frame into his swivel chair, shook his head several times and seemed to drift off. After some thought he said, 'What beats me is how nobody there heard nothing. Where was Dave Lee Nelson?'

'Asleep. He came running across the yard in his

underwear when Becky's screams began raising the roof.'

'Will, I see your dilemma. Assuming your ma was wide awake, if a stranger walked in with you in the next room, she'd've commenced hollering – and that didn't happen.'

He reached down to slide open a drawer, inserted a lean hand and brought it out with two jolt glasses on his fingers, reached for the half-full whiskey bottle on the shelf behind him and poured two large measures. He slid one to Will Sagger, tossed back the other, and sighed.

'That leaves your pa walking in – either on his own, or with somebody. I'd go for the second alternative – but if that's the way it was, who did your pa bring into his home, and what the hell happened in there?'

'I've spent two days thinking about it,' Will Sagger said. 'If there's an answer, it's buried deep.'

McLure had his finger poked into his empty glass. His lips were thrust out as he absently moved it over the desk's scarred surface.

'Man rides out,' he said softly. 'Everyone goes to bed except Mary Ann. Nobody hears a damn thing. Then Becky's screaming, and Mary Ann's dead. . . .' He looked up, head cocked quizzically. 'We don't know for sure your pa came home, do we?'

'We don't know anything, for sure.'

McLure swore softly. 'No, and if he didn't come home that leaves Mary Ann keeping as quiet as a mouse when a stranger walks into the house and approaches her brandishing a knife – and now we're going round in circles, that idea already chucked out with the rest of the garbage.'

McLure waited, thought some more, then slapped his hands flat on the desk.

'Will, is there anything you're not telling me?'

Sagger eased back in the flimsy wooden chair, rocking almost imperceptibly in his contemplation so that the loose frame creaked, creaked, creaked. . . .

He realized that, since talking to Cree and McLure, his snap judgement of the happenings at Bar C had developed more holes than an old tin colander. The clear picture of his drunken pa taking a knife to his ma and hightailing had been swept away – had to be, for sanity to prevail. In its place he could see stark black and white images that came and went in flashes like stormy scenes briefly revealed in the flicker of sheet lightning: a black-clad stranger sneaking in under cover of darkness, knife glittering; his pa riding in with an old pal after a night's carousing, a chance meeting degenerating into something wicked; his pa again, this time watching white-faced and helpless while an old enemy cut his wife's throat, then being forced, at gunpoint, to ride away with the killer.

Who? Why? What in the name of God had gone on, two nights ago, when death visited the Bar C?

'Will?'

Blinking, he jerked back to reality, to the present.

'No.' He shook his head, yet even as he did so he was remembering that one lasting image that had stuck with him for the whole of the two days and suggested to him, from the beginning, that his pa was leaving a message. It was nothing, yet it was every-thing, because for the man who was Daniel Sagger it was completely out of character – but, at that moment, it was not something that Cliff McLure needed to know.

'No,' Will Sagger said again, 'there's nothing else.'

CHAPTER THREE

Most days Red Keegan kept customers out of his saloon until Lou, the one-eyed, gammy-legged swamper had grumbled his way around dim room and sunny plankwalk with his head at a permanent tilt, a broom jabbing like a spear with careless disregard of passers-by and a bucket of soapy water ready to drench those the broom had missed.

That morning Jake Cree crossed the street first and leaned over to whisper in Lou's ear while Will Sagger slipped by on his blind side. Then, with a wink and another sly word that drew a grudging smirk from the cantankerous old fellow, Cree followed Sagger.

Still troubled by Cliff McLure's final question and his own less than honest answer, Sagger walked straight across the room and slapped a hand on the bar. Red Keegan emerged from the shadows at the rear with his jaw jutting aggressively, took one look at Sagger's face and served up a glass of cool, foaming beer. A second followed as Cree approached the bar, and Keegan stepped back, wiping his hands on his apron.

'Well? How'd it go with McLure?'

Sagger downed half his drink, set the glass down, and looked at the gunsmith.

'About like you said. A lot of questions. Precious few answers from me that gave him any more than you got.'

Cree snorted. 'Some would say you're playing your cards a mite too close to your vest.'

Drinking, shrewd eyes watching Sagger over the rim of his glass, Cree let the double-barrelled meaning in his words hang threateningly for a moment while Sagger mulled them over and Keegan watched impassively from the sidelines. Then Sagger slammed his drink down hard enough to slop beer.

'Godammit, Jake!' he said fiercely. 'That's my right. *My* ma's dead and buried, *my* pa's gone missing, and right now what I'm doing is trusting to *my* judgement. Maybe what's bothering me is I'm looking at a grain of sand and seeing a mountain, so before I jump in with both feet I'd like more to go on.'

Red Keegan cleared his throat.

'Your pa was in here two nights back.'

In the sudden silence, Sagger glanced around quickly as the swing doors flapped and two men walked in and crossed to a window table, registered this sudden arrival of Texas Dean and Beebob Hawkins and felt a prickling stir of unease, then turned again to Keegan.

'Go on.'

The burly, red-haired saloonist's eyes were cautious. 'First, I need to know what's going on.' He, too, glanced away at the newcomers before returning his gaze to Sagger and raising his eyebrows.

'Hell, it's no secret. You've been standing there, you've already heard most of it.' Sagger looked down, fiddling clumsily with the wet glass. 'Two nights ago is when it happened. Becky came through to the living-room, found her ma with her throat cut. Pa had gone out earlier that same night. He's not been seen since.'

'That's it, in a nutshell,' Cree said. 'Enough to prod your memory, Red?'

'Nothing wrong with my memory,' Keegan said, and he reached for a jug, topped up Sagger's glass. 'I'm sorry to hear about your ma, feller, but I had a pain in my guts just watching those two sittin' with their heads together and—'

'Two?'

'Your pa and a mean-looking feller with pistols tied down, wearing clothes and a hat looked like they'd been picked off a Mex' rubbish tip when the buzzards had been and gone. Hell, I could smell him from here, and your pa—'

'This feller have a name, Red?' Cree said.

'He spoke to Sagger and no one else, and I never saw him before that night,' the saloonist said bluntly, biting off the words, and his eyes flicked across the room and back and suddenly were defiant.

'You scared of those two dummies?' Cree had raised his voice, and now he put his glass down carefully, watching Keegan's eyes.

23

'Easy, Jake,' Sagger said softly.

'Too many people being too tight-mouthed sticks in my craw,' Cree said, still loud, and across the room a chair scraped.

'You mind explaining that there comment,' Beebob Hawkins called, 'to a couple of fellers settin' minding their own business?' His voice was a lazy southern drawl. The chair had been his, and now he circled the table and came across to the bar with the graceful walk of a dancer, his colourless eyes curiously pale in his sun-browned face. Behind him, Texas Dean had already stepped sideways away from the window table, and now the unshaven gunslinger with the gaunt look of an undertaker drifted silently to the end of the bar.

'We've had a killing out at Bar C, a good man gone missing,' Cree said, 'but when questions get asked, people're so close mouthed they're likely to starve to death.' He'd turned away from the bar, and had Dean on the edge of his vision as he spoke to Hawkins. His apron had been discarded in his workshop, and over his serge pants he wore a gunbelt holding an engraved, nickel-plated Colt .45 with carved ivory grips. A modern model designed for a dandy, perhaps, Will Sagger thought, but here worn with pride by a craftsman who could use it to shoot the pips out of a playing card at twenty paces.

Beebob Hawkins had moved closer. His head was tilted, his pistol worn high and on the left side, butt forward, but it was the bony, big-knuckled hands that drew Sagger's gaze for the white crescents of old scars told of countless barroom brawls.

'People bein' close-mouthed,' Hawkins repeated softly, and his eyes narrowed. 'Not yet clear enough, Cree.'

'Will Sagger is holding something back – but his ma's dead and from a grieving man I'd expect reticence. He needs help. Red's not telling all he knows – and for that, I blame the demeanour of you and your partner.'

At the end of the bar, black-clad Texas Dean's cold laugh was like a death rattle. 'Hell, we're two tough lookin' customers all right. But nobody's close-mouthed, 'cause there's nothing to tell. A man rides in from Hole In The Wall and Daniel Sagger goes back to his bad old ways, that's the beginning and the end of a dull story—'

'You're lying!'

'And you're still wet behind the ears,' Beebob Hawkins snarled at Will Sagger, and he stepped around Cree, planted a big hand on Sagger's chest and slammed him back against the bar. Cree stepped swiftly away from the bar with his hand at his hip, but in turning to face Hawkins and Sagger he put Texas Dean behind him – and every man froze at the oily click of a pistol's hammer.

'Lift your hands, move back against the shelves, Red,' Dean said, and the big saloonist lifted his hands from the scattergun under the counter with a sibilant hiss of anger. Dean nodded satisfaction, moved his pistol to cover the gunsmith. 'Cree, why don't you mosey on over to your shop and maybe oil a few guns while Beebob clears this up?'

'I'll wait.'

'Out.' The pistol waggled. 'And stay away from Cliff McClure.' Cree hesitated, glared at Red Keegan, tossed a glance at Will Sagger that was unreadable then turned and went out through the swing doors.

'Smooth as silk, Texas,' Hawkins said, and turned back to Sagger. 'Now, where had we arrived at?'

'You were blackening my pa's good name.'

'Why, that was Texas doin' that, but I guess I share his views,' said Hawkins.

'And now you're going to eat your words.'

'Hell, he was tellin' the truth, Sagger. That poisonous-lookin' feller Red couldn't put a name to was Amos Skillin, but he's only one of several rode down to Ten Mile in the past weeks to twist your pa's arm.'

'He's right,' Red Keegan said.

'But not about the reason,' Sagger said.

'Ain't give you the reason,' Hawkins said. 'Told you your pa's arm got twisted once too often and this time he went along, but I'll be damned if I said why.'

'Something about his bad old ways?'

'Goin' back to them's *what* he did, not why he did it. Why, hell, everyone knows Daniel Sagger moved up to Wyoming back in the seventies because there was no place left for him to hide—'

Sagger hit him.

He half turned, then slammed a foot down and whipped his right fist round in a swinging hook. His fist cracked against Beebob Hawkins's cheekbone. Pain knifed to his elbow as the big man stumbled backwards and fell across a table. Sagger went after him in a flat dive. He landed atop the downed man, grabbed his shirt front with both hands and slid with him to the floor as the table splintered.

Hawkins exploded. Like a cat, his stringy muscles seemed to expand in all directions as he twisted his lean frame and reared free. As he did so, his hard fists rained bruising blows on Sagger's face. Dribbling salty blood, pawing at the air, Sagger fell away from the savage attack. His shoulders slammed into the sawdust. He kicked out wildly. His right boot drove like a piston into Hawkins's groin. The lean man recoiled, yowling and spitting.

Sagger spun, and went after him. His shoulder sent a table flying. Doubled over in agony, Hawkins took Sagger's heavy assault on his broad shoulders. Then the man's big hand shot up and fastened in Sagger's hair. It clamped tight, tugged. Fiery pain flared as Sagger felt his scalp begin to rip. He grabbed the man's wrist and hung on as he rolled over Hawkins, landed flat on his back with an agonized grunt. Hawkins shifted his hand. It landed like a broad claw over Sagger's mouth and nose, and Hawkins pushed down hard. Grinning, he levered himself to his knees behind Sagger. His weight ground Sagger's head into the sawdust.

Snuffling, struggling to draw ragged breath against the horny palm, Sagger hung on to the man's wrist and doubled at the waist. Both feet swung over in a fast, overhead kick. His boots slammed into Hawkins's face and he heard the crunch of bone. He released the wrist. The hand slid away.

A roll brought him on to his knees, chest heaving. Hawkins was on hands and knees, head hanging, spitting blood and splintered teeth. Without looking at Sagger or lifting his head, he snapped a hand across his body. It came back fast, clutching a six-gun. The barrel whipped sideways, cracked across Sagger's jaw. At the back of his eyes, lights flashed like stars against a flaming red sky. His head rang. He crumpled face down in the sawdust, and Beebob Hawkins came down heavily astride his back.

'That's enough!'

The hand that had clamped on Sagger's shirt collar slowly relaxed. He twisted, rammed an elbow into the big man's ribs, broke the weakening grip and threw him clear. When he looked towards the doors, face slick with blood, eyes unfocused, he didn't need to see the tall shape outlined against blue spring skies, or the shotgun that was cocked and deadly to know who had roared the warning.

Squinting through his agony, Will Sagger grinned happily.

'Good of you to join us, Dave Lee.'

CHAPTER FOUR

'So tell me: were Beebob Hawkins and Texas Dean being their usual ornery selves – or is there a whole lot more to this than anyone's lettin' on?'

Will Sagger was leaking blood on to the floor of Cliff McClure's office over by the gun rack. Dave Lee Nelson was in the corner propping up the big iron safe, and looked more than equal to the task: his wide shoulders were threatening to split his faded cotton shirt, and his massive head with its mop of blond hair and drooping dragoon moustache looked hard enough to drive fence posts.

On the street side of his desk, McLure was standing well back from the sound and the fury.

He'd been out doing his rounds at the other end of Ten Mile Halt when the fracas developed in Keegan's. The first he'd known of it was when he caught sight of Beebob Hawkins's bloody mask as he whipped his bronc down the centre of the street, then jumped smartly back on to the plankwalk when a sneering Texas Dean cut his horse in close enough to catch him with one stirrup and kick dust in his face.

Tight-lipped, McLure had rubbed his hip and looked the other way to watch Sagger and Nelson enter his jail office, followed them at a slower pace to allow his anger to subside, then come close to being blasted back out into the street by the ferocity of Sagger's verbal attack.

Now, he let what appeared to be Sagger's closing question hang like a bad smell in the suddenly silent room, then came away from the door and dropped into the flimsy wooden chair.

'Maybe,' he said, 'you should say what you mean.'

'Goddammit, McClure, you know what I mean. Red Keegan's behind his bar with his mouth all puckered like a dried grape and his eyes shifty. Beebob Hawkins is scattering insults like a man sowing corn, and it looks like I'm the only man around here still in the dark – except for Dave here, who's also the only man so far to lift a finger to help.'

McLure sighed. 'First off, a man has to help himself, Will – and you ain't doin' that.'

Hotly, Sagger said, 'You've no damn right—'

'I've every right. You say your ma's dead, your pa missing. All that tells me is two decent people suddenly ain't where they should be, and when their son walks in here talking of killing, and pushing his weight around, then my suspicions—'

'Jesus, are you suggesting—?'

'Knock it off!'

The sudden silence was like that following a thunderclap. Will Sagger clamped his teeth, glared fiercely at McClure, then used his arms to lower himself gingerly into the marshal's swivel chair. Across the desk, McClure held his gaze. Sagger was aware of Dave Lee Nelson, a towering figure to his left with the shotgun alongside him, tilted against the safe. His silence was . . . what? Accusing? His way of willing him to listen to McClure, to open up to him?

Sagger leaned forward. Blood dripped on to the desk. He scrubbed it with his sleeve, brought the sleeve up to his bloody mouth. Still looking down, he said, 'Pa's got a Winchester .44-.40. Model of 1873. He won it in a sharpshooting contest at a Texas county fair.' He looked up, met McClure's level gaze. 'It's still on its hooks, back home.'

McClure thought a moment, then nodded slowly.

'Where this is going seems about as hard to get a fix on as a single snowflake in a blizzard. So, tell me, is this what you've been holding back?'

Sagger nodded.

'Your pa wouldn't do that, is that what you're saying? He wouldn't ride out without his '73 Winchester?' He shook his head. 'Hell, boy, assuming you've been telling the truth about that night, we just don't *know* what went on. Could be any number of reasons your pa left his rifle behind, first one springing to mind being he had no damn choice.'

Sagger pursed his lips, then winced and dabbed with his bandanna at the fresh flow of blood and continued to look at McClure, waiting.

'So,' McClure went on, more gently now, 'if you don't go along with that notion, are you saying that rifle being there means your pa's dead?'

'The rifle's mine,' Sagger said, 'when Pa dies. I guess you know he came home for good when I was ten years old. What you maybe don't know is he brought that rifle with him, wrapped in a torn old army blanket. In those early years we sat and talked, winter nights mostly, by the fire. Ma'd be in bed, and he'd take the rifle down off its hooks, let me hold it, squint along the sights, firelight dancing on the barrel all hard and shiny, him talking real soft and distant. About how ownership hadn't come easy. How he'd earned that rifle the hard way—'

'What did he mean?'

Sagger shrugged. 'What he said: he won it in a shooting contest against tough opposition at a county fair, and that story never changed. That's what I believed, then, that's what I believe now . . . I . . .' He dabbed at his lips, said softly, 'Then the talking stopped, as time passed, and I grew up and he taught me to shoot and then ranch work took over and it's twelve years since that day he rode into the yard. . . .'

'Get to the point, son.'

'For as long as I can remember he's been telling me, when he dies, that rifle passes to me with his blessing – only, since he started drinking—'

'How long's that?'

'A month. No, less. Hell, I don't know for sure.'

'But every night since he started soaking it up,' Dave Lee Nelson said in a gravelly voice, 'and on nights when you've not waited up, kid, I've more than once helped your pa over to the bunkhouse to get his head down so your ma could sleep easy.'

McClure turned sharply to the older man. 'He do any talking?'

'Wild talk. Nightmare talk. I paid no heed.'

Nelson met McClure's gaze of frank disbelief with a faint smile, and the marshal bit back his obvious irritation and looked at Sagger.

'Yeah, go on, Will.'

'I've been there most times,' he said, with a sharp glance at Nelson. 'A couple of those nights when he's come home late, worn out, unsteady on his pins, he's sat at the table in the lamplight with his head in his hands, kinda mumbling. And what he's been saying is maybe the rifle ain't coming to me like he's always said, nice and easy, handed down father to son. Maybe I'm going to have to earn it, like he did, and that's set me wondering. . . .'

Silence settled over the room. Nelson wandered away from the safe to the window. McClure set the chair creaking as he drifted away into deep thought and, with a glance at him, Will Sagger slid open the drawer, located the jolt glasses and reached behind him for the whiskey bottle. He was pouring a shot for himself and the marshal when the door banged open and a dusty man with a battered hat and run-over boots came in from the street.

Slim Gillo was taller and leaner than McClure, looked like a starving scarecrow likely to be pulled off balance by the weight of his deputy's badge, and was as sharp as a whole family of foxes. McClure acknowledged his arrival with a nod, absently reached for the glass Sagger slid across the desk, then realized what he was doing and pushed it away again with a grimace.

'Time for coffee, not hard liqour,' he said, with a glare at Sagger, and the lanky deputy took in the room's occupants with a swift glance, then crossed to the stove and hefted the coffee pot.

'Been talking to Red Keegan,' he said.

'More lies,' Will Sagger said softly.

Gillo was rattling tin cups. He cast a withering look at Sagger.

'Red's in a bind,' he said. 'His loyalties lie in one direction, his business interests are tellin' him to keep his mouth shut or face the consequences.'

'Those being?'

'According to Red, who's had more than one earthy conversation with Beebob Hawkins,' Gillo said to McClure, 'if he talks too freely his saloon will finish up as a pile of charred, smouldering wood.'

'Such talk should be reported.'

'It has been. In confidence.' And, as the deputy commenced slopping coffee into four tin cups, there was a warning look of deep solemnity on his long, lean face.

'What else did Red say?' McClure said, accepting a steaming cup. 'In confidence, of course,' he added, for the benefit of the other listeners.

'Both Beebob Hawkins and Texas Dean have rode with that stinkin' bundle of rags, Amos Skillin. They know him well, they're afeared of him – and, know-ing those two hard bastards, that's a sobering thought. Anyway, it seems Skillin's been sendin' his outlaw cronies down regular from Hole In The Wall with the aim of takin' Daniel Sagger back with them. Why, Beebob couldn't or wouldn't say, but those owlhoots were ordered to take him, one way or another. To that end they began by askin' him real nice, over the weeks and maybe half a dozen weari-some rides down from the hills. It moved on to some hard, impatient talk that turned threatenin', and maybe even involved violence that Daniel Sagger was able to handle. But when nothing those owlhoots could throw at Daniel looked like workin', why, Amos Skillin rode down from the hills hisself, and he acted.'

'Acted how?'

Gillo was sitting on the steps leading to the cells, all arms and legs, tin cup held in both bony hands. He shrugged.

'According to Beebob, Skillin used a woman and a little girl to get his way. That's all he knows, or is will-ing to let on.'

'I guess,' Cliff McClure said, with a sideways look at Will Sagger, 'we can fill in the rest of the story with-out Beebob's help.'

For Will, the bits and pieces coming from Beebob Hawkins and his sidekick had added to his own hazy reading of the weeks' happenings, the mention of a little girl being used telling him how a ragged outlaw who had lost patience with the hard men he rode with had come down from Hole In The Wall to plumb the depths of cruelty.

Had it been done by guile? Will Sagger could see no other way. Somehow, Amos Skillin had walked from Red Keegan's saloon with his arm around a drunken Daniel Sagger's shoulders and talked the rancher into taking him into his home. The ride from Ten Mile Halt had been under the stars, Daniel's thoughts – if his head was clear enough – probably of nothing more than sharing a hot supper. At Bar C, Skillin had found Mary Ann Sagger in her night clothes, waiting up for her man, and with one swift stroke of a razor-sharp knife – the drunken man alongside him bewildered and helpless at the speed of the attack – he had cut the woman's throat and revealed the extent of his treachery.

In the sudden, terrible silence, all that would have been heard was the ticking of the clock, perhaps the soft sound from the adjoining room of a sleeping girl's slow breathing. The woman lay dead in a slick pool of blood and, as her husband looked on in horror, the man with the bloodstained knife in his fist grinned savagely and with the fingers of his other filthy hand struck off the only two alternatives.

That same bloody knife gets used on your daughter.

You go with me now.

'What could he do?' Will Sagger said hoarsely, as the images swamped him with emotion.

'The best he could, the only thing he could do, in the circumstances,' said Cliff McClure. 'Over the

36

weeks, he did the groundwork by warning you of trouble ahead. On that night, he left his clear message.'

'A '73 Winchester,' Sagger said.

'For a young man to earn,' McClure said. 'The hard way.'

CHAPTER FIVE

Four men rode back to Bar C.

They rode at midday when the sun was bright and warm but the air still holding the crisp freshness of a Wyoming spring. Two, Will Sagger and Dave Lee Nelson, were riding home. A third rode with a duty to perform, a lean and dusty man with a battered hat and run-over boots and the badge of authority that was to be a form of protection; a battered tin emblem that would glint in the sunlight and cause those who saw it from afar to have second thoughts.

According to Cliff McClure.

With the reputation of the infamous outlaws who used Hole In The Wall as a refuge already unsettling his stomach, Deputy Slim Gillo doubted that, but McClure had a young deputy able to fill in, and Gillo wasn't paid to think. And Cliff McClure had threatened to slam young Will Sagger in a strap-steel cell for his own protection if he didn't agree to Gillo riding along.

The fourth man had closed shop, selected the finest rifle from his rack and, with the fancy six-gun at his hip and a paper package tied behind his saddle, brought his frisky roan gelding dancing out of Ten Mile Halt's livery barn to tuck in behind Slim Gillo.

Jake Cree, the gunsmith, was taking flowers to a grave and going looking for an old friend.

The hour's ride passed mostly in silence, each man alone with his thoughts as he allowed his horse to drift into a position on the trail that would avoid the worst of the dust.

Nelson, realizing Sagger did not wish to be disturbed, ignored the young man riding alongside him and deftly rolled a cigarette that lasted for a number of miles before being flicked into a creek.

Gillo stayed alert, his eyes scanning the far horizons. Cliff McClure had expressed the opinion that, with two days passed, Amos Skillin and Daniel Sagger would be long gone – but he'd been wrong before and Gillo figured he'd be shirking his responsibility if he took the marshal's word as gospel.

In cattle terms, Jake Cree rode drag, stoically enduring the dust from the three riders ahead of him while he squinted sideways at the distant purple smudge that was the southern tail of the Bighorn Mountains, the fainter line of Owl Creek Mountains further to the west – and Hole In The Wall.

That last – a notch in the mountains leading to a hell hole inhabited by cold-blooded killers who considered themselves the Robin Hoods of the West – he couldn't see, but as he looked ahead to where Will Sagger rode alongside his foreman, the gunsmith knew that out of sight was not out of mind.

Young Will Sagger was casting too many glances across his left shoulder, his eyes squinting too intently into the far distance. Hole In The Wall was dominating his thoughts. The kid was impatient to ride.

They gathered in the living-room at Bar C, each man averting his eyes from the hideous dark stain only partly covered by the Indian blanket thrown down days ago by Will Sagger. The house was empty. Becky had been taught at home by Mary Ann and, in the days since the killing, Will had found neither the time nor the inclination to give thought to her schooling. Now he knew she was off somewhere on the open range, a young girl alone with her piebald pony and an aching heart but watched over closely by Bar C hands, and as he looked at Cree he knew the gunsmith was sharing his thoughts.

'Cath will look after her,' Cree said.

Quickly, standing with his back to the big stone fireplace and mantel over which the gleaming Winchester '73 rested on padded iron hooks, Will Sagger arranged for one of the hands to take the girl into town and deliver her safely to Jake Cree's wife where she would remain until Sagger's return. Nelson would stay on at Bar C, hire men for the spring roundup, buy in thirty or more horses for the remuda, haul the heavy chuck-wagon out of the barn for a check over and ensure that the day-to-day ranch work continued without a hitch.

Jake Cree and Slim Gillo would ride with Will Sagger.

'And with the easy decisions taken care of,' Sagger said, 'we've got some hard planning to do. I reckon a pot of hot coffee might make thinking easier.'

But Dave Lee Nelson, understandably disgruntled at being left out of the chase, was ahead of him, the big foreman already in the kitchen rattling pots. What he had to do in there took no time at all: Becky had breakfasted long after her brother rode out, the stove was still hot, the coffee bubbling. When Nelson came through, four brimming cups balanced on a square of timber, the aroma of the java filled the room instantly and with its familiarity pushed the horror of what had happened a little way into the background.

'This is the way we all figure it, I reckon,' Sagger said, 'with a lot of help from Slim there, and his talk with Beebob Hawkins.' He took one of the cups, drank, gathered his thoughts and emotions, and went on, 'Amos Skillin rode down from Hole In The Wall to talk to Pa. Two nights ago he came riding out here – with Pa – stayed long enough to complete his bloody work then lit out, taking Pa with him. If we're right, then we've got the name of the killer, and we know where they've gone.'

'What we don't know, is why the hell it happened,' said Slim Gillo, a gaunt figure outlined against the bright window as he sipped his coffee.

'Which, if you'll excuse my bluntness,' Jake Cree said, from the comfort of a deep chair, 'makes not a blind bit of difference. We're gathered here to plan how we go after Daniel Sagger. If we want answers, that's the only way we'll get them.'

'Good points, all of them,' Sagger said. 'Slim's

right, we don't know the reasons for what went on. And Jake, I reckon your arrow hit home when you said it makes no difference. What we do know is we've got Beebob Hawkins and Texas Dean scared of Amos Skillin—'

'What we've got is me *sayin'* those two are afeared of that renegade,' Gillo said, 'and maybe I'm right. But either way, I suspect them of bein' hock deep in this mess – maybe forced into it by that ugly renegade and his evil crew – and if we bear that in mind we won't get any rude shocks.'

'More wise words,' Cree said. 'With those two unpredictable bastards already gunning for Will, keeping one eye on our back-trail makes a lot of sense.'

'If you fellers are so darn clever,' Dave Lee Nelson said, 'when are you going to get to the point?'

Cree chuckled softly. 'I can see why Daniel made you foreman, Dave. I guess we've trampled back and forth over the main issue without once putting a boot on it hard enough to hold it down.' He leaned forward to place his empty cup on the table. 'So, what about it, Will?'

'Well,' Sagger said, 'that's two of my closest friends telling me bluntly I'm sitting wasting time drinking hot coffee when we know who's going, where they're going, and why. You're both right. We're going round in circles. The only thing we don't know is what happened here, and we find that out by talkin' to my pa. So, Dave, I reckon getting to the point means deciding when to go. And the best time to go is right now.'

Nelson nodded his satisfaction and again headed for the kitchen. 'I'll fix up some provisions, fill a couple of canteens for each man.'

'Me,' Jake Cree said, 'I'll go run my eyes and hands over the horses, check the boxes of shells I picked up in a hurry on the way out.' He looked at Sagger, said softly, 'I know for sure I packed a couple of boxes of .44-.40.'

Sagger nodded. He watched the little gunsmith go out into the sunshine and clatter down the steps to where the horses were tethered, then turned and, with feelings akin to reverence, took down from its hooks the shining Winchester '73. This, he knew, would need no scrutiny, no last-minute checks. He was cradling it in both hands, but could smell fresh oil; and when he slid his hand around the stock and worked the lever, the movement of the empty breech was smooth, the metallic click softened by lubrication lovingly applied by Daniel Sagger.

And that, Will Sagger realized, was just two days ago. How many more days would it be before he saw his father again? Would he ever again see him alive? And, alive or dead, what violence would he, Jake Cree and Slim Gillo encounter before the puzzle of a brutal killing was solved, the reason for one man's slide into heavy drinking and flight to the devil's cauldron that was Hole In The Wall finally understood?

His bruised and bloodied jaw clamped tight to bring on the pain that drove those desolate thoughts from his mind, Will Sagger turned away from the stone fireplace with his father's rifle in his hands and strode across a packed dirt floor stained with blood to begin a ride into uncertainty, and danger.

CHAPTER SIX

Midday. Clear blue skies, the sun directly overhead, no breath of wind to cool the skin.

They'd pulled off the trail to rest the lathered horses, tethering them close to a shallow pool fringed by coarse grass and flattened to a glassy sheet by the scorching heat of that spring day, then sunk down in the scant shade beneath the trees to smoke a cigarette and stare their separate ways into the limitless distances.

Amos Skillin, a renegade clothed in filthy rags with wild eyes rolling under a battered sombrero, twin pistols tied down, a battered Sharps carbine in a saddle boot and his rough hands and the huge Bowie knife in its fringed scabbard still stained rusty red with a woman's blood.

Daniel Sagger, a lean, dignified man with a single Smith & Wesson Schofield at his hip, a man who, on a rainswept night, had ridden home drunk from Red Keegan's saloon in Ten Mile Halt to be torn apart by grief and rage.

Had been. He was able to say that now with feelings approaching exhilaration for, in two days and through searing pain that exploded from whiskey-fogged memories of his terrible frailty and his wife's savagely mutilated body, something had happened to Daniel Sagger. Loath though he was to concede that it had taken tragedy to bring about the return of integrity and manhood – to bring him, like a steer caught at the end of a tight rope, snapping back to his senses – he knew that two days on the trail without the spurious escape offered by Red Keegan's cheap liquor had cleared his mind, sharpened his senses, and prepared him mentally and physically for the forthcoming battles.

As he pulled on his cigarette and listened absently to the movements and the crude hawking and spitting of the renegade who had taken Mary Ann's long hair in his filthy hands and hissed like a snake as he cut her throat, Sagger could feel the strength singing through his body, could look ahead with an alert mind unfogged by strong drink or confused thoughts. And he needed that clarity. For there would be battles, and bloody ones, against foes as yet unnamed and others who were ghost riders emerging unexpectedly from a hazy past. It was a past he had ridden away from twelve years ago. One of the ghost riders was a former *compadre*. And still he did not know why that old trail partner needed him. . . .

'Another day,' Skillin said, the harsh voice cutting through his thoughts. 'Another day too long when all this could've bin finished weeks ago without any blood spilled.'

'Finished?' Sagger rolled over and came to his

feet, sending the cigarette hissing into the flat pool. 'To be finished there has to be a start, and I've been told nothing.'

'All you need to know.'

'Wrong. In a month I've been driven half crazy by men bringing terse messages from Cajun Pride. *That* was finished, the two of us ridin' the owlhoot, and it seems after twelve long years it still hasn't sunk in. We were together, then we split. That was final.'

'You split.'

'Same difference.'

'Until now.'

'Why now?'

'That's up to Cajun.'

'And what about you?'

Skillin was up off the ground now, his stubbled face turned to Sagger, the weight of his pistols tugging at his loose gunbelt as weirdly out of kilter eyes looked the other man up and down with undisguised contempt.

'Yeah,' he said, with a challenge in his grating voice. 'What about me, now?'

'I think what happened back there was a maverick losing patience and going berserk. You weren't getting your way, the long shadow of Cajun Pride was like a black storm cloud threatening to burst over you and, like a rabid dog, you went plumb crazy.'

'So?'

'You were acting on your own, the Cajun Pride I knew would never condone what you did – and what happens to rabid dogs is, they get a bullet in the head.'

'You think you can do that? You think you can pull your iron fast enough to put a hole in my head?'

'Fast enough?' Sagger's laugh was mocking. 'There's a while to go, and I don't think you can stay awake long enough to stop me.'

'Yeah, but nothing's changed,' Amos Skillin said, eyes rolling, face contorted with insane glee. 'If I die, your little girl—'

'Everything's changed.' Sagger snapped the words. He took a fast stride forward, clamped one hard hand on Skillin's right forearm and with the other took a bunched fistful of shirt front, thrust out his head so that his face was inches from the rene-gade's grimacing countenance. 'You had me over a barrel. I was a weak fool too drunk, too damn slow, to stop a crazy bastard from slicing my wife's throat. But, as drunk as I was, I could see that bloody knife in your murdering fist glittering wet and red and I knew that unless I got you out of that house, and fast, then the next to die would be my beautiful little Becky.'

Sneering, Skillin jerked his arm from Sagger's iron grip, pulled his shirt free and stepped back. 'She'll still die—'

'How?'

'Beebob and Texas. Back there in Ten Mile Halt. And they know what to do, when to do it . . .'

For an instant, Daniel Sagger was silenced. Then his thoughts raced, he recovered, and he said, 'No. Back there it was your deck, your deal. I played the hand your way, you won the pot. But now I'm deal-ing, and in this game you're on your own and if I shoot you dead there's nobody to know, nobody to care, nobody likely to go back to Bar C and risk his neck committing murder on the say-so of a dead man.'

'Then I'll drop you now, where you stand,' Skillin snarled.

'Do that. Make your play. But if you drop me, what then? Do you ride on without me, face Cajun Pride's rage?'

For a long moment the hot still air was electric, both men as tight as coiled springs, right arms bent, fingers flexing. Then Skillin straightened, shook his head, made a half turn.

'Maybe,' he said, with sly, sideways glance, 'Cajun Pride ain't the man he used to be.' And then he spat into the pool, turned his back on Daniel Sagger and walked to where his horse was standing hip-shot, dozing in the heat.

Maybe he isn't, Sagger thought, watching the filthy renegade tightening the cinch and climbing into the worn saddle. Cajun Pride had been a hard man, a fast gun, a reckless fool who chased pretty women and other people's cash and looked back to roar with mocking laughter at the posses floundering on his trail. But if that buccaneering spirit had grown weary, if Cajun Pride had hung up his guns, Sagger thought – then what in hell's name does he want with me that's so important he sends a messenger like Amos Skillin?

It was an unanswerable question, and it stayed Daniel Sagger's hand. In the cold and wet of a hideous night, he had ridden with Amos Skillin to pull him away from Circle C, his sacrifice had put Becky out of immediate danger, and no man would condemn him if he now used his six-gun on the murderer to exact a terrible justice. But that would not be the end of it. Cajun Pride seemed driven and tormented by a terrible desperation, the dead Skillin would be replaced by another hard man, then another, and the danger would return tenfold. The only course open to Sagger was to ride on and confront his old *compadre* – and when he came to that decision he was comforted by the conviction that the gleaming Winchester '73 he had left resting on its hooks would speak to young Will Sagger far louder than any words, and bring the boy in hot pursuit.

He would ride like the very devil, and he would not ride alone. And as Daniel Sagger climbed into the saddle, the half smile that lingered on his face sent Amos Skillin into a rage that was like a stick of dynamite on a short fuse hissing dangerously between the two men.

CHAPTER SEVEN

'What they're doin',' Red Keegan said through his teeth, 'is goin' after Will Sagger's pa. Now, if you ain't got the brains to work that out for yourselves—'

'When?'

'Hell, they rode off to Circle C to pick up supplies; if they moved fast they're most likely gone by—'

'How many?'

Behind his bar, furiously wiping a glass to keep from hurling it at Beebob Hawkins, Keegan glanced across to the table at the back of the room where Texas Dean was idly playing solitaire, then back at the coiled figure of Hawkins.

'Figure it out,' he said tightly. 'You cross the road to get your gun fixed, you'll find Cree's door locked. Walk down the street and ask McClure where you can find Slim Gillo, you'll get a blank look.'

'Those two? That long streak figures he's a deputy lawman? A gunsmith old enough to be my grandpa?'

'Them, and Will Sagger.'

Hawkins sneered. 'A kid, carryin' a fancy rifle makes him a man.'

Keegan stopped wiping, narrowed his eyes. 'That's right, a Winchester '73 – but how do you know that?'

Without answering, Hawkins swung away and strode to the table at the back of the room. Texas Dean watched his approach, swept the cards together then tossed the deck on to the table where it scattered, spilling cards on to the sawdust covering the dirt floor. He filled the two jolt glasses, slid one to Hawkins as he sat down, watched the tall man with the scarred knuckles and the cross-draw outfit as he downed the drink.

'Gone?'

'Likely. But that don't matter. Circle C's due north. We head north-west we'll cut them off.'

'I heard you talkin'. An old man, an excuse for a deputy and a kid wet behind the ears – right? But what if Dave Lee Nelson's with them, maybe a couple of Circle C hands?'

'No. They'll be lookin' after the kid, makin' damn sure nobody gets near her.'

Dean shook his head, his eyes glinting. 'The kid's in town.'

Hawkins, absently playing with the scattered cards, went still. He thought about what Dean had said, about the possibility of Dave Lee Nelson and the Circle C hands riding with Will Sagger. Keegan had figured on three men riding after Daniel Sagger, but he could be wrong. If he was wrong, the odds were unfavourable, and he and Dean needed something to give them an edge.

'Where in town?'

'Cree and his wife live over the shop. A while ago

a buckboard pulled up outside.'

'Let me finish for you,' Hawkins said. 'It was Dave Lee Nelson and the girl – and they went inside?'

'Close. The girl, but with one of the Circle C riders.'

'But he didn't stay?'

'Buckboard left soon after. . . .' Dean shrugged, waited.

Hawkins again fiddled with the cards, flipping a king, a knave, the ace of spades. His eyes were on the unshaven, black-clad rider across the table, but his mind was roaming the sun-drenched prairie, seeing two men, tired and dusty as they flogged their horses towards the smudge of hills to the west; behind them – a long way behind – three men riding hell-for-leather. That was what he'd envisaged, but now . . .

'Texas, what you saw tells me a couple of things,' he said. 'First off, it wasn't Nelson brought her in so, yeah, he could've ridden with Sagger, Cree and Gillo like you said. That shifts the odds their way somewhat. But, second off, if that Circle C rider did head back to the Sagger spread, then there's only Cree's wife watchin' over the kid.'

'If that's the way it stands,' Texas Dean said, 'then wherever Nelson is he'll be figurin' a job's been well done, Will Sagger will be chasin' after his pa believin' he's got no worries back home—'

'When, in truth,' Hawkins said, 'they're just pipe dreams because right now we've got the chance to snatch ourselves one mighty sweet hole card—'

And, breaking off in mid-sentence, Beebob Hawkins snatched at the scattering of loose cards and with a flick of his powerful wrist sent them skimming across Red Keegan's saloon.

Tow-headed and petite, Rebecca Sagger was a young girl who hid surprising wiry strength in a small, slim frame. She had ridden her first pony almost before she could walk, and had always enjoyed donning faded denim shirt and pants and helping out at branding times. Not, Cathy Cree recalled with amusement, that the little girl had done much more than run about looking busy amid the dust and bawling calves and sweating, good-natured Circle C cowboys – but everything Daniel and Mary Ann Sagger had taught her or allowed her to do had prepared her for a life that was rewarding, but uncompromisingly tough.

Now, watching the tow-head ten-year-old eat her supper, Cath Cree patted her own greying hair somewhat nervously and wished, as she had many times that afternoon and evening, that Jake had remained behind. She had a loaded Smith & Wesson Pocket .32 revolver within easy reach on the dresser, but she was not happy with the arrangements worked out by her husband and Will Sagger and felt that, if they had been left to a woman, they would have been very different.

If Will Sagger believed Becky was in danger, why entrust her to the care of a middle-aged woman? Why move the grieving young girl from the familiarity of her home, when Circle C was a good hour's ride away from the ruffians hanging out in Ten Mile Halt and, there, she would have her own room and the round-the-clock care of Dave Lee Nelson and the other tough cowboys?

And, once again, why, why, had Jake ridden with Will Sagger? Common sense told Cath that Dave Lee Nelson was the man for that job, one of the other cowboys could have taken over the foreman's job while Nelson was away, but instead of that an elderly gunsmith had taken it upon himself to act as body-guard, guide, mentor, and the Lord knew what else.

Well, Cath thought, it's far too late now to grumble. . . .

'Bed for you, Becky, as soon as you've finished.'

Becky nodded. She'd finished eating the beef and vegetable stew and had pushed her plate away, but Cath knew she was listening to the noise exploding through the swing doors of Red Keegan's saloon across the street – coarse laughter, the occasional tinkle of a glass breaking, the hard high shrill of a woman's voice; sounds that would be new and exciting to a young girl accustomed to the night-time silence of an isolated ranch.

Lips tight, Cath went to the window. She'd left it open during the heat of the day, but now with darkness upon them she pulled it to, reached for the curtains – and stopped.

A cigarette glowed in the shadows at the back of the opposite plank walk, a little way down from the saloon. When Cath narrowed her eyes and allowed them a few seconds to adjust she saw Beebob Hawkins and Texas Dean.

They were watching her.

And even as she returned their gaze – even as she

57

stepped to one side of the window, heart thumping – they came out of the shadows and set out across the street. An alleyway ran down the side of the gunsmith's premises, and the exterior stairs to the living quarters were on that wall. But Hawkins and Dean were crossing at an angle, heading away from Jake Cree's shop.

'Aunt Cath, what's wrong?'

'Nothing. Nothing's wrong.'

Quickly, realizing fear had caused her to speak sharply, she pulled the curtains across and turned to the young girl with a forced smile.

'Nothing at all,' she said in a softer voice. 'I was just thinking that the noise from Red's is going to stop you sleeping.'

'I'll be fine.'

'Of course you will. Now, you run along and get ready for bed while I clear the table.'

The living-room door closed behind young Becky Sagger. Cath Cree stood looking at it, frozen. Fear came screaming back like a wild animal, tearing at her throat, bathing her in perspiration. Her legs had turned to water. Ears straining for every faint sound, she forced herself to move to the table, forced herself to gather together the dishes.

But their clatter blocked out other sounds.

Terrified, she left them alone. Listened.

Through the thin door the clink of washbasin and jug, the splash of water. From the street, even through the closed window, the hubbub from the saloon.

And footsteps.

'Oh, no,' she moaned.

Somebody was in the alley, climbing the outside stairs. Their booted feet were heavy, thudding on the treads. There was no attempt at stealth, and for an instant that gave her reassurance. Then she was stricken by despair, and panic. Wildly, her gaze flew to the dresser, the gleaming revolver. Her hands were fluttering at her apron, wiping away grease, twisting, turning. She opened her mouth to cry out, to warn Becky – but her throat was dry, and all that emerged was a rattling croak.

The footsteps had stopped.

No, not stopped; she'd imagined them.

A smile pulled at stiff lips – and she swore softly, forced her legs to move her across the room to the dresser. She picked up the revolver, felt the cold, heavy metal; turned to face the door.

They had stopped, of course. They were at the door, now, listening. If *she* listened hard, she would hear their hoarse breathing: Beebob Hawkins and Texas Dean.

With both hands, Cath Cree gripped the pocket pistol and her thumb pulled back the hammer. She lifted it. Pointed it towards the door. Tried, in vain, to still the trembling.

And a boot slammed against the door and it exploded inwards in a shower of white splinters that rained on the two armed men who burst into the room.

CHAPTER EIGHT

'Two days' start on us,' Will Sagger said. 'We could ride like devils, end up with spurs drippin' blood and horses dead on their feet – but we won't catch Skillin and my pa. So what we've got to figure out is, how the hell do we bust into Hole In The Wall when the best lawmen in the West have admitted defeat – and what do we do if we make it, ride into that hell-hole and come up against Cassidy's Wild Bunch? They're not going to take kindly to us bein' there, even if our business doesn't concern them and we turn a blind eye.'

'Maybe,' Jake Cree said, 'we should think of today and leave the rugged times ahead to take care of themselves.'

Sagger grunted, tossed a pine log on the fire and watched the sparks fly into the dark canopy of trees to scatter and die amongst the leaves; listened to the hiss and crackle as the flames hungrily took hold of the resiny wood; felt the chill on the side of his face as the night breeze cut in from the river, the icier chill deep inside that came from fear for his sister's safety, and of the unknown.

Slim Gillo was dozing, a still figure cocooned in blankets with his head on his saddle and glazed eyes half closed as they stared unseeingly up into the darkness. A cigarette glowed between his fingers, and suddenly he spat a curse and fiercely shook his hand as the glowing tobacco burned down to sear his skin. Awake now, aware of what had broken into his dreams, he came up on an elbow and looked sheepishly towards the two men at the fire.

'Coffee still hot?'

'What's left of it.'

Cree poured what was mostly grainy black dregs into a cup, rose from his log and carried it across to the deputy, then returned to the blazing fire.

'Will's worrying about what lies ahead.'

'And behind me,' Sagger said. 'Cath will look after Becky, I know that – but in town they're too close to Hawkins and Dean and that puts your wife and my sister in danger.'

'One day at time's tough enough,' Cree said, 'without dwelling on tomorrow's troubles.'

'The troubles ahead I can handle, it's the ones I left behind that bother me.'

'We decided town was the safest place for Becky, planned it that way, went ahead and did it. Now leave it be.'

'She's my kid sister, Jake, and I've got a terrible foreboding—'

'If trouble arises Cath's armed, and tough enough to handle it one way or another.'

Gillo swung to a sitting position, elbows on knees,

both hands clasping the hot cup.

'If I spoke like that, Cliff McClure'd take away my badge for bein' an optimistic fool.'

'You didn't look like you were doin' too much planning.'

'He's got it all figured,' Will Sagger said. 'That right, Slim?'

'No, it ain't. But I did some cogitating in the saddle, and it seems to me no self-respectin' bunch of owlhoots would associate with the likes of Amos Skillin. So this talk of the Wild Bunch—'

Will looked at Cree. 'We thought you were asleep, Slim.'

'A good lawman,' Gillo said, 'never rests.'

Cree chuckled his appreciation. 'So you reckon this feller who's almighty keen on having Will's pa come up and talk to him is no Butch Cassidy, no Kid Curry, just some over-the-hill owlhoot lookin' for . . . lookin for what, exactly?'

'Past glory. Easy money. I've gone part way, now you tell me.'

'Pa never talked about his past in front of us kids,' Will said, 'but there was a time, some years back, when I almost caught him out.' He hesitated, gathering his thoughts, remembering with more ease than he had expected but forced to dig deep for details grown hazy with time. 'It was night, something woke me, a big clap of thunder maybe, and I came charging out of the bedroom when he was talking soft and low with Ma by the flickering light of the fire. If I'd been quick, quieter, I could have held back behind the door and listened. That way, I'd have got the whole story. But I was half asleep and scared and I barged straight in, so all I got was a name and then he clammed up and Ma bundled me back to bed.'

'This is the first time you've mentioned a name, Will.'

Sagger looked at Cree, smiled wryly. 'So already something good's come out of Slim's cogitating and your musing. That name stuck with me: Cajun Pride—'

'The Utah Kid.'

Sagger and Cree exchanged glances, then looked across at Slim Gillo. He levered his gangling frame up off his blankets, ambled over to the fire and sat on a log with his arms and legs all over the place and his hands spread to the flames.

'Comes of having piles of yellowing Wanted dodgers atop McClure's safe and nothing else to read,' he said. 'Cajun Pride, the Utah Kid, wanted for robbery down in southern Texas. I figured he'd be dead by now, plugged by some stinkin' bounty hunter in a Mex cantina, or caught and strung up by a mean posse.'

'Hold your horses,' Sagger said cautiously, 'all we've got is a name from the past.'

Cree shook his head. 'It's something we can get our teeth into. We know from Slim this Pride was an outlaw, and you heard your pa telling your ma about him on a stormy night not too long after he rode home for good. There was a connection then, so why not now?'

'In that case, wouldn't Pa be on one of those dodgers?' Will looked enquiringly at Gillo. 'Did you come across any bearing the name Daniel Sagger?'

'None that I can recall,' Gillo said. 'The one I saw with Pride on was going back, oh, twenty years or more. The picture was a bad one, but even then this Utah Kid was no spring chicken.'

The fire spat and crackled. Gillo again climbed awkwardly to his feet, lifted the coffee pot out of the flames with the help of his folded Stetson and walked off into the darkness to where water bubbled from a cluster of rocks. The coffee pot rattled as he filled it from the spring. When he returned and placed it hissing over the flames, the badge on his vest glinted in the firelight.

Watching him, Jake Cree said, 'Maybe Daniel Sagger was a lawman. That might link him to the Utah Kid and, if it is Pride up there at Hole In The Wall, it'd explain why he'll stop at nothing to get ahold of your pa.'

For a while, Will said nothing. All three men were listening to the blackened coffee pot as it came to life and began to sing, their eyes drawn by the hypnotic flickering of the flames, their senses lulled by the warmth and the lateness of the hour. But a different kind of warmth was enveloping Will Sagger. Since the discovery of his mother's body he had been tormented by a terrible fear. He had watched his father transformed from a clean-living rancher and family man into an unshaven drunkard, and when he disappeared leaving behind his murdered wife, logic told Will that there could be but one answer: Daniel Sagger was an evil man who, after twelve years of toeing the line, had returned to his evil ways.

The one jarring note was the shiny Winchester '73 left hanging on its hooks. And now the wisdom of Jake Cree had come up with this: a lifeline, a feasible explanation that was so obvious it was impossible to see how it had been missed; the answer to all their questions that in a flash cleared Daniel Sagger's name and explained his mysterious past, and the puzzling present.

'Thanks, Jake,' Will said softly.

'Not now, not yet,' Cree said ruefully. 'Because if your pa was a lawman who tangled with this Utah Kid in the past, I can see only one reason for his bein' dragged up there to Hole In The Wall – and that's the Kid harbourin' some crazy notion of revenge.'

CHAPTER NINE

Cliff McClure was behind the desk in his office talking to well-oiled Dave Lee Nelson when they heard the distant snap. For an instant the sound was so faint, so insignificant, it failed to register. Then, as his subconscious went to work deep down, memories of other times and other places were stirred, rose to the surface and – still talking inconsequentially of this and that – he recalled a bone-thin gambler on a Missouri riverboat, an irate miner accusing him of cheating, a pale hand sneaking beneath a frock coat's tails and the brittle snap of the shot that settled the argument—

'That was a shot from a pocket pistol,' McClure said, and sprang from his chair to reach up to the wall-hook for his gunbelt.

Nelson, who had ridden into town to see how Becky was getting on then stayed for a rare evening of relaxation, had sobered up fast, ripped the door open and was out in the street and running. McClure charged out after him, still buckling his belt, and the two men ran at an angle across the street to where the lights from the saloon spilled across to shine on the locked door of Jake Cree's gunsmith's shop.

From the lighted, curtained upstairs windows there was no sound. They raced into the dark alley. Drawing his gun, Nelson began clattering up the steep stairs. Behind him, pistol in his fist and cocked, McClure saw that the door to Cree's home gaped wide. Even as they climbed towards it, a child screamed shrilly, and Nelson let out a roar of rage.

Immediately, a voice from inside the room yelled, 'Stay back, we've got the woman!'

Nelson stopped on the small, square upper landing, flattened himself against the wall alongside the door, looked back helplessly at McClure.

'That was Beebob Hawkins,' McClure said softly. He took another cautious step upwards, held the rail as he paused with his rear foot still on the lower tread. 'Texas Dean'll be in there with him. Tell them you're coming in, but first you'll throw in your pistol.'

'And then?'

'You're alone. If they see you're unarmed, they won't keep the woman covered. Then keep them talking, work it so they're standing with their backs to the door. When the time's ripe . . .'

Turning his head, Nelson hoarsely called out his name and what he was about to do. McClure couldn't hear the reply, but Nelson took a deep breath, moved away from the wall and with an underhand throw sent his pistol sliding across the unseen room's board floor. Then, with a mute glance down the steep stairs at McClure, he stepped into the room.

Mumbled talk, the words indistinguishable, the sense unimportant. All McClure knew was that Dave Lee Nelson was playing his part by keeping the two roughnecks occupied. That gave the lawman the slimmest of chances – but a slim chance was better than no chance, because without his intervention the woman and the young girl faced unimaginable horrors.

A stair creaked as McClure stole upwards.

The talk stopped, left a heavy silence, then picked up.

He reached the small landing, hesitated with the toes of his boots touching the pool of lamplight flooding from the room; watched that light on the boards, the gross, elongated shadows, from those shifting shapes tried to determine the position of Nelson, the woman and the girl, the two men.

And shook his head at the impossibility of the task.

Inside the room, Beebob Hawkins said, 'We aim to stop Will Sagger, so his kid sister's going with us.'

'Where is she?'

'Ask *her*.'

'Mrs Cree?'

'In the other room, Dave, getting herself ready for bed.'

McClure smiled savagely. Dave Lee Nelson was using his head, asking questions that drew the right answers and painted a picture for the listening lawman. The girl was still out of the way. Cath Cree was there, in the room – but it must have been her pistol they'd heard, and if Nelson could get his hands on it, or snatch his own pistol from the floor when

McClure exploded into the room . . .

But had the Circle C foreman managed to ease past Hawkins and Dean while he was talking? If McClure burst into the room and the two villains were still facing the door, even a cocked six-gun would be of little use. He'd get one man, but not the other – yet there was only one way of finding out for sure what was going on in there. He had the one chance, the agonizing spin of a coin, the uncertain turn of a card, and he was playing blind when the odds against him were heavily stacked.

Aware of cold sweat beading his forehead, a tightness in shoulders and chest that made the drawing of each breath a terrible effort, Cliff McLure braced himself, lifted his six-gun, and took that uncertain, fateful step out of the shadows and into the lamplit room.

Amos Skillin was baiting him.

They'd pulled off the trail on to a slope of tumbled rocks and stunted mesquite as the sun dropped behind the western mountains, lit a smokeless fire of dry sticks, cooked up a meal and brewed coffee in Skillin's blackened pot. Now, with the moon a thin crescent rimming the high still clouds with silver, the filthy owlhoot was sprawled on his blankets with the Mexican sombrero tilted over his eyes, drinking from an unmarked bottle of moonshine corn whiskey and muttering insults.

'You tell me,' he said, 'why the hell the Utah Kid is keen to ride with a man with a yeller streak down his back who's walked out on him once already.'

'Pride was past it, a liability,' Sagger said. He was sitting on a flat boulder, watching the half-drunk killer across the dying fire. 'There's a thin line between success and failure. Riding the owlhoot, failure means someone dies. When one man loses his fine edge, he puts others in danger.'

'Excuses, not reasons.' Skillin tilted the bottle, drank, belched. 'Justifyin' what you did, when what you did was you turned your back on a good man, a fast gun, twice the man—'

'Older, slower, his sights set too high and refusing to admit—'

'A man the equal of Jesse, better'n Curry, smarter than Cassidy—'

'This afternoon you were suggesting Pride was past it.'

'Past his best is still better than almost any other owlhoot.'

'How the hell,' Sagger said, 'would you know?'

Skillin lifted the bottle, squinted past it at Daniel Sagger, then carefully placed it upright in the dirt. As he struggled to a sitting position, it tipped over. Whiskey gurgled, slopping on to his boot. He kicked out, sent the bottle rattling away into stones lost in the darkness outside the circle of firelight. Squinting blearily, he struggled with a tied-down holster, pulled the pistol to the front of his thigh.

'Because,' Skillin said thickly, 'me and the Utah Kid're like that.' He lifted a hand, held the first and second fingers upright and crossed one over the other. 'That's why he sent me, knowed he could rely on me, knowed I wouldn't let him down like

71

goddamn Cold Hand Sagger, yeller-streak Sagger, useless bastard walked away from him, stands by while his wife's throat—'

Like a cat, Daniel Sagger came to his feet and sprang away from the fire. Amos Skillin's out-of-kilter eyes followed him, and a savage grin bared yellow teeth. As time stood still and Sagger dropped to a crouch with his hand hovering over his six-gun, he knew that a drunk Amos Skillin was still as dangerous as a striking rattler. The man spent half his life swilling moonshine whiskey. With his mind dulled by mountain liquor he would still draw like greased lightning, instinctively send hot lead screaming to its human target.

But in that moment that seemed to stretch to cover all eternity, Sagger knew that Amos Skillin, the grinning, sneering Amos Skillin, was a dead man. He'd gone too far. A superhuman strength surged through Sagger. The muscles of his right arm sang with power. The distance between his clawed fingers and the butt of his six-gun shrank to nothing so that, before he exploded into action, he could feel the smooth wood against his palm and the cold trigger hard against his curled finger.

In that instant when time slowed to a crawl, Amos Skillin went for his pistol. And a detached Daniel Sagger watched. He saw the renegade tilt his body sideways to free his right arm. Saw the filthy hand stab towards the holster lying on stained pants. Saw the pistol pulled clear, a stubby thumb draw back the hammer, the glittering barrel lift—

Sagger shot him.

His six-gun was in its holster. Then it was in his hand, spitting fire. A black hole appeared beneath Amos Killin's chin. His eyes flew wide. His mouth gaped. He tried to speak, but the words gargled wetly in his throat. Then he fell backwards, his head slamming against his saddle, bright wet blood bubbling on his lips.

Daniel Sagger dropped to his knees, bowed his head, felt the damp earth beneath him and the electric tremor tingling through every nerve in his body. 'The only way, it was the only way, the only way, the only way. . . .' The words hammered at his brain, he knew they were sensible and true – but what had he done? He had executed a killer – but by so doing had he put his daughter in danger?

Numb, drained, Sagger climbed to his feet and put away his six-gun. And it was as if those movements, ordinary movements, the return to normality, cleared his mind. He had done nothing to endanger his own existence, or the lives of those he loved. The action that had taken but a split second and removed a cold-blooded killer from the face of the earth would have caused no stir beyond the shrinking circle of the fire's light. If Will was coming after him, he would be too far back down the trail to have heard the shot. And what he, Daniel Sagger, had said to Amos Skillin that afternoon held good now more than ever: back in Ten Mile Halt there was nobody to know, nobody to care, nobody likely to go back to Bar C and risk his neck committing murder on the say-so of a dead man.

But his actions had created a dilemma.

Sagger was now free to return to his ranch, nurture the grieving members of his family and throw himself into the back-breaking work coming up with the spring: the hiring of hands, purchase of a remuda, the roundup and the branding and the long cattle-drive to market. But if he did that, over his head there would still be hanging the unsolved mystery of Cajun Pride. He had thought things through to the inevitable conclusion earlier that day: the dead Skillin would be replaced by another hard man, then another, and the danger would return tenfold. Now, Skillin *was* dead, and what he had envisaged would surely become reality.

So it was a dilemma, but one that was easily solved. He was now a free agent. If he continued on to Hole In The Wall to face the man who had been his companion in crime, it would be because he wanted to go, not because he was being forced. It would be because he wanted to move any present or future dangers that might threaten his family – and for that reason alone there was but one way out of the dilemma.

An hour later, Amos Skillin's body lay buried beneath a pile of rocks, and Daniel Sagger had broken camp and was riding through the night towards the distant mountains.

'Stand still!'

The impact of Cliff McClure's roar hit Beebob Hawkins and Texas Dean like a physical attack from the rear, brought them spinning around. They moved fast, but not fast enough: Nelson had walked in and they'd caught him cold and dropped their guard but now they were unnerved by the shock of the unexpected and their attention was fatally distracted. Dave Lee Nelson took his chance. As they turned sluggishly to face the new danger, he swooped low to scoop up his pistol. Cath Cree, too, had been forewarned of what might happen by glances Nelson had cast in her direction. She had been expecting intervention from the same quarter, had anticipated McClure's sudden appearance, and when Hawkins and Dean found themselves caught in no-man's-land between the six-guns of the Circle C foreman and Ten Mile Halt's marshal, she calmly stepped over to Beebob Hawkins and snatched her Smith & Wesson pocket pistol from his belt to make it a three-way bind.

'Unbuckle them,' McClure said to the stunned pair. 'Let them fall, then step aside.'

Hawkins's pale eyes were fathomless. He looked at Texas Dean, then unbuckled his gunbelt and sent it clattering to the floor. His black-clad sidekick did the same, glared at McClure and angrily kicked the gunbelt across the room. The heavy weapon slammed against the interior door. As it hit the wood-work, the young girl in the other room whimpered in fear, then broke into uncontrollable sobbing.

'Cath, you attend to Becky,' McClure said. 'It's all over. There'll be no more trouble, this night or any night.'

He watched Cree's wife, still holding her pistol, leave the room and close the door quietly behind her. Then he turned to Hawkins and Dean.

'What the hell were you thinking? Big fellers like you, what crazy idea turned you into cowards going after helpless women?'

Beebob Hawkins turned his head aside and spat.

Dave Lee Nelson said, 'They know Will Sagger's gone after his pa. I guess they figured gettin' ahold of his kid sister would make him change his mind.'

'Muddled thinkin',' McClure said, shaking his head. 'How would taking his sister back here in Ten Mile Halt prevent him riding across country to Hole in The Wall?'

'Because he wasted too much time at Circle C,' Hawkins said. 'Ridin' across country, we'd cut him off.'

'With Becky slowing you down?' McClure considered for a moment, then nodded. 'Might have worked, but that still don't say why. What the hell's goin' on at Hole in the Wall that's so all fired important it requires Sagger's presence there?'

Hawkins grinned. 'You know about Daniel Sagger, who he is?'

McClure looked at Nelson, saw incomprehension and concern in the big foreman's eyes, and said, 'It's my job to know. I know what he's been in the past, and what he is now. Everybody in town knows he put that past behind him when he rode home, but now it looks like continual harassment and the cold blooded murder of his wife has turned his head – and one way or another I aim to find out what's going on.'

'Sending Slim Gillo along with Will was a step in that direction,' Nelson said – a statement, not a question, but when he looked at McClure for some reaction, the marshal had already moved on.

'Dave, what Hawkins said made sense. If he could intercept Will with Becky slowing him down, you could do the same only a damn sight faster.'

'Why should I do that?'

'Because when he pokes his nose into that hornet's nest called Hole in The Wall, he's goin' to need all the help he can get.'

'He left me to look after the ranch, keep an eye on Becky.'

'Forget it. With these two behind bars, his sister's safe. You give me a name, I'll ride out to Circle C and tell the man you nominate he's actin' strawboss.' He paused, looked hard at the big Circle C foreman, the erect posture, the clear eyes, and came to a decision. 'I'll also swear you in, pin a badge on your vest.'

Nelson hesitated. Listening hard, he could hear no sounds from the other room. The little gunsmith's wife had comforted and reassured Becky Sagger; the young girl was in good hands here, and there was a man out at Circle C who could organize the run up to a spring roundup without raising a sweat. And, much though Nelson respected Jake Cree and Slim Gillo, he knew that his presence alongside them would add considerable power to a small force that was setting out to achieve the impossible.

It would need strength, determination and luck to bust into Hole in the Wall – and the more Dave Lee Nelson thought about it, the more he thought about what had happened to Mary Ann Sagger and tried to put himself in Daniel Sagger's place, feel the savage emotions that must be tearing the man apart – the more he wanted to be in on the attempt.

'All right,' he said. 'I'll ride after them, and I'll wear that badge with pride. Let's get these two locked up and I'll be on my way.'

CHAPTER TEN

The silence was eerie. In the valley, the waters of the meandering creeks tumbled and sparkled in the sun, the tule grass on the slopes leading to the sheer, thousand-foot-high red cliffs to the north of the basin gleamed like polished brass. Far away, the opening to the narrow gorge that was the entrance to Hole In The Wall was a black notch shimmering in the heat of midday.

Nothing moved.

Cajun Pride, the man who many years ago had ridden north from Louisiana to forge a reputation as the Utah Kid and, years later, an unholy alliance with Daniel 'Cold Hand' Sagger, turned away, hiding his disappointment behind a gaunt mask of a face in which his black eyes were deeply sunk. He moved away from the outcrop that had been his vantage point, stumbled once over a loose rock, then made his way across the stretch of naked earth that fronted the log cabin.

Two men watched his approach. Fergel O'Brien was a bulky figure at the window. Karl Weiss, dark and brooding, had moved away from the solid timber table still littered with greasy eating utensils and empty coffee cups left over from breakfast and was in the open doorway. There was a critical expression on his bearded face, uneasiness in his watchful gaze. He had noted the way that Pride – dark hair streaked with grey beneath his flat-crowned black hat, flamboyantly dressed in yellow shirt beneath a black vest – had turned from his vigil with an almost imperceptible loss of balance; how he had stumbled over the loose rock that, not too long ago, he would have stepped over without looking.

'No sign?'

It was a needless question. The entrance to the gorge was as clearly visible from the cabin as it was from the outcrop fifty yards away and, with the aid of field-glasses, O'Brien had scanned the distant ravine and reported to Weiss: no movement; no riders; Amos Skillin was not bringing Daniel Sagger back to Hole In The Wall.

'He'll come. *They'll* come.'

Pride's voice was thin, lacking in strength, but, as he answered Karl Weiss's question, there was a fire smouldering in his black eyes. The strength of that gaze forced Weiss to take a step backwards, and he shrugged as the smaller, leaner man brushed past him and dropped into a chair.

'All right,' he said, 'maybe they will. We're expecting too much, too soon. Ten Mile Halt's one hell of a ride, and Skillin's an old man. . . .'

O'Brien chuckled at Weiss's crude attempt at humour, came away from the window and put the field-glasses on the table.

'Maybe they will, maybe they won't,' he said. 'But my argument still holds good: why bring in a man who's been on the right side of the law for a dozen years? A mile up the creek there's the finest owlhoot guns, the Wild Bunch: Robert Leroy Parker, Harvey Logan, Elza Lay—'

'No!' The fire in Cajun Pride's eyes had turned to fury as he hitched at the worn six-gun on his hip, and that fury was directed at Weiss. 'I don't give a damn for those fellers, under any name. Call them Butch Cassidy, Kid Curry, call 'em what you like and it makes no damn difference. It's me wants the Union Pacific's Overland Flyer. *We'll* take it together, just like old times, the Utah Kid and Cold Hand Sagger, one last job—'

'With help from me and O'Brien?' Weiss said.

'Sure. Of course. You know this, you rode out a week ago, talked to those fellers up in Buffalo, they'll be here any day now.'

'And together we'll get this job done?' O'Brien said. 'Never mind those others, they're cavalry makin' up the numbers, here to pick up the scraps we leave – because this is the big pay day, right, the pot of gold we snatch before you die?'

'Sure, and maybe we'll both die, me and Daniel Sagger. But what a way to go out, a blaze of glory, the Adams Express car taken by two old timers – by the best.'

O'Brien sat down, shifted greasy tin plates, toyed with the field-glasses. 'Maybe Sagger, if and when he gets here, will figure that glory ain't worth dyin' for.'

'Too many maybes,' Pride said dismissively. 'Maybe this, maybe that. Hell, of course we don't know. So we wait and see what happens, what the man decides when he gets here, listens to what I have to say. But it's when, not if. He'll get here, today, tomorrow, and I have this dream, this vision, and I know Daniel Sagger and he'll want in and you two, you can be a part of it—'

'I was up there last night,' Weiss cut in, 'with the Wild Bunch. We had a few drinks, played some hands of poker, but the talk was mostly about a fortune in bonds and cash carried by the Union Pacific. Butch Cassidy's got his eyes afixed on that train, mentioned the town of Wilcox.'

'So we move fast, beat them to it.'

'Stop the train where?'

'The name Wilcox came up, you say, and that sounds about right.'

'Same train, same place? You know what Cassidy will do to me?'

Pride's smile was cold and distant. 'With all that cash in your saddle-bags, you won't be coming back, Karl.'

For a long moment there was a tense silence in the small cabin. Karl Weiss knew Cajun Pride had a death wish, and he was pretty damn certain he knew why. But what Pride yearned for was his business. Other men were not prepared to die – would do anything to avoid that fate. Weiss had teamed up with Fergel O'Brien because they were caught cold by the *Rurales* and had ridden out of Mexico spurring their horses and ducking their heads in the same hail of gunfire. They were lucky to be alive. A spell with the outlaws holed up in Robber's Roost had seen them splash across Green River and ride north to Wyoming and Hole In The Wall, and they'd moved into Cajun Pride's cabin down-slope from the Wild Bunch's headquarters to gather strength for the long push to the Canadian border.

It hadn't worked out that way. Cajun Pride was silver-tongued, persuasive. His ideas were big, but to see them to fruition he needed alongside him hungry, reckless men with fire in their bellies and, as Weiss pointed out when discussing it with O'Brien, it would make a sweet end to their owlhoot days if they could cross the border into Canada with saddle-bags stuffed with cash.

But that had been three months ago, and since then everything had turned sour. Pride had begun wasting away before their eyes, his mind kept flipping backwards to the old days, he spent more and more time on his own and suddenly he was obsessed with the idea of one final job with Daniel 'Cold Hand' Sagger riding stirrup.

And that was where his thoughts tailed off. There had never been any mention of the aftermath, of what they would do when the job was finished. Until now. 'With all that money, you won't be coming back', he'd said to Weiss; but when he said it there was a wistful, almost painful look in his eyes, and Weiss was intelligent enough to know that there was more than one way of not coming back and the one Pride was contemplating was something Weiss wanted no part of.

'Rider coming!'

O'Brien was back at the window, his shout cutting though Weiss's thoughts and sending him lunging for the door. His eyes snapped towards the distant entrance to the gorge, squinted through the heat haze – and he saw him. A single rider. Out in the open, the distance cutting his movement to a beetle's crawl as he came down from the gloomy notch in the rocky walls that made Hole In The Wall an impregnable stronghold, and out into bright sunlight.

'It ain't Skillin,' O'Brien said. 'I'd know that filthy bastard anywhere.' He had the glasses to his eyes. He lowered them, turned as Weiss came back inside. 'Just the one feller, I ain't seen him before – so how the hell did he get past the lookout?'

They both looked at Cajun Pride. Stiffly upright on the hard wooden chair, not bothering to look towards the window, there was a fierce light burning in his black eyes and on his bony knees his thin hands were clenched into fists.

'Daniel "Cold Hand" Sagger,' he said. 'He's come, like I knew he would. I don't give a damn about Amos Skillin; he was the last chance, the last throw of the dice, but whatever happened back there in Ten Mile Halt, it's brought Sagger running – and now we can get down to planning the

robbery of the Union Pacific: one, brilliant, auda-
cious robbery that'll make our names known all
over the West and set Daniel and you two fellers up
for life.'

CHAPTER ELEVEN

'There'll be lookouts, eagle eyed, with long rifles to pick us off at a distance,' Slim Gillo said. 'So either we look for another way in – and as far as I know there ain't none – or you've got a white flag handy, a long stick to tie it on, and one hell of a plausible tale to tell.'

'The way I see it,' Jake Cree said, 'there'll be one man perched up on the rocks and he'll be hungry and thirsty and so damn peeved settin' out there starin' into the sun he'll welcome the sight of *anything* that moves.'

Will Sagger grinned, discarded the wet piece of grass he'd been absently chewing, and said, 'So we'll say the truth lies somewhere down the middle. One sentry, alert because he knows he's a dead man if anyone slips past him, but not prepared to shoot until he establishes identity. He'll have glasses, and he'll use them from time to time. But he'll be relying on a trail of dust to pinpoint intruders, and seein' as we got here under cover of darkness and kept our heads down. . . .'

The three men were off the trail, their grazing horses loosely hobbled, the low north-south ridge on the western side of their overnight resting place giving them cover from that distant lookout while providing them with a clear view of the outlaw stronghold if they inched up to the crest. All three were on that crest, down on their bellies and squinting through the tall grass that nodded in gentle waves before the warm breeze. Now, as one, they wriggled backwards then climbed to their feet, the gangling deputy leading the way down to where saddles and bedrolls were scattered around the blackened rocks encircling the ashes of the dead fire.

'We still ain't decided,' Jake Cree said, 'why Daniel didn't turn back when he'd plugged the man who murdered his wife.'

'Or even,' Slim Gillo said, 'if he did turn back and rode straight past us when we were bedded down snorin' our heads off. In which case, we're goin' to be walkin' into the lion's den and maybe gettin' our fool heads blown off for no damn reason.'

Will Sagger said nothing. He busied himself tying his bedroll, saddling up, scattering rocks and kicking dirt over the remains of the fire, but all the time his mind was active as he recalled stumbling across a pile of rocks fifty miles back, the remains of a man lying stinking beneath it with blackened blood staining his shirt front and wild eyes rolled backwards in their sockets to stare whitely at the searing skies.

Even now the memory of that discovery filled him with perverse pleasure, and his heart swelled with emotion as he imagined his father with the killer in his sights, his finger squeezing the trigger, the dazzling muzzle-flash and the soggy thud of the bullet slamming into Amos Skillin's grimy throat.

But that pleasure came and went. It was something he savoured when he was rocking to his horse's gait and dozing in the saddle, or rolled in his blankets savouring a last cigarette as he gazed up at the time-less stars. And it was something apart, a son's appre-ciation of an execution carried out by his father, Daniel Sagger, and done – Will was convinced – with complete justification and as casually as a man would swat a fly. Sagger had removed Amos Skillin without compunction but, unless the killer had talked before he died, Daniel Sagger would be no nearer to under-standing the reasons behind his murderous actions. He had done no more than kill the messenger, and so Will Sagger was convinced that his father had not turned back, but had ridden on to confront whatever awaited him at Hole In The Wall.

'All right, looks like that's us ready to go,' Jake Cree said, the little gunsmith's familiar, resonant voice cutting through Will Sagger's thoughts. 'We're all saddled up, those high cliffs guarding Hole In The Wall are no more than a mile to the west, and there's a sentry settin' up there just waitin' for some-thing to happen.'

Having deliberately planted those disturbing thoughts, Cree looked hard at Slim Gillo, hunkered down picking his teeth; at Will Sagger, standing by his patiently waiting horse cradling his father's gleaming Winchester '73. That rifle rarely left his hands. When it did, it was either tucked into the soft leather saddle boot under his right thigh where he could feel it constantly, or deep inside his blankets where the heat of his body warmed the glistening metal and kept its oiled mechanism in smooth working order – ready for instant action.

'So what's it to be?' Cree said, as the silence stretched without drawing any comments. 'Three goddamned musketeers riding in as one to scare the living daylights out of that lonely owlhoot up there, or one of us riding in alone to test the water? – and, though it might have been said in jest, if you think about it that white flag on a stick isn't such a bad idea.'

'It has to be me,' Will said. 'It's my pa we're trailing, it's only right when the time comes it's me sticks his neck out.'

'What's the thinking behind that offer?' Slim Gillo said. 'You figure your pa knows you'll come after him, maybe handed out tin-types so those trigger-happy outlaws don't shoot you on sight?'

'I think he'll have said something, yes.'

'Yeah, but as the lawman sent along to make sure you don't do nothing foolish,' Gillo said, 'I'm forced to oppose that plan of campaign. In any case, pure common sense tells me it won't work. If you make it through that notch, me and Jake could be sittin' out here until winter without knowing if you're alive or dead. An' iffen you don't make it, what the hell am I going to say to Cliff McClure?'

Standing with both forearms resting on his saddle, looking across the patient horse at the other two men, Sagger grinned mirthlessly. 'That last sounds like you're considering your safety, not mine,' he said, and drew an appreciative chuckle from Jake Cree. But while the morbid jesting could lighten the tension, it could do nothing to solve the dilemma Sagger faced. They'd pushed their horses hard for a hundred miles, rarely discussing what lay ahead but sticking blindly to some unspoken agreement about getting there fast and riding straight into the outlaw stronghold. When faced with the awesome rock barrier and the narrow cleft that could all too easily be guarded by one man with a rifle, the lack of planning suddenly looked stupid, and dangerous.

Sagger lifted his hands, spread them in a gesture of helplessness and came away from his horse.

'Common sense tells me to wait for nightfall. But knowing my pa's ahead of us by two clear days and already in there with those hellions screams at me to push ahead, whatever the risk.'

'If darkness gives us the best chance,' Cree said, 'we should have gone in last night.'

Gillo shook his head. 'About the only thing we've agreed on since leaving Circle C is that last night we were too bone weary to risk a confrontation with this Utah Kid.'

'Sad, but true,' Jake Cree said. 'We'd mulled over the idea Daniel Sagger might once have been a lawman. Then we halfway decided if he wasn't a lawman he was an outlaw riding with the Kid. If the first's right, then maybe the Kid's got some notion of revenge. But if he was an owlhoot. . . ?'

He spread his hands, looked from Gillo to Sagger.

'There's no answer that's entirely right or wrong,'

Will Sagger said, 'and anyway we're wasting time. I'm going in.'

'All right,' Slim Gillo said uneasily, 'but listen hard to this. We're kinda bogged down here, no place to go in daylight without bein' seen, but we've got an option. This ridge gets higher a little ways to the north, and there's a scattering of trees giving better cover. So me and Jake'll move up there, wait around. But if we ain't heard from you in twenty-four hours' – he looked at Cree for approval, got it, turned back to Sagger – 'we'll come after you – so if you do find your pa and maybe come across this Utah *hombre*, you make damn sure things're sorted out one way or another.'

'Cliff McClure couldn't have put it any clearer,' Will Sagger said, 'and knowing you two are backing me up makes the ride in that much easier.' He saw the glint of pride in the deputy's eyes, the almost imperceptible straightening of his lanky frame, and grinned. 'Heck, by the time I finish telling them about the posse that's waiting on the plain to pull me out of there, every owlhoot at Hole In The Wall will be eager to throw down his guns.'

With a final glance at the two older men who were both gamely trying to hide their misgivings, he returned to his horse, swung quickly into the saddle and rode away at an angle across and up the ridge. When he went over the top he looked back once, caught the quick farewell flick of Jake Cree's hand and swallowed hard as he pointed his horse towards the open plain and the daunting barrier of high cliffs.

It was still early, the sun bright but not yet hot enough to disperse the pockets of mist that lay untouched by the mild breeze in shallow basins and sharply defined rocky clefts. It was through this scarred, barren landscape that Will Sagger rode, not hurrying, keeping his horse to an easy trot and all the while scanning the cliffs that lay ahead of him and in particular the break in them that gave the outlaw hideout its name.

The rock faces and summits on either side of that infamous notch appeared so naked that it was difficult to see where a man with a rifle could hide. But Will Sagger had done enough riding in his ranch work at Circle C to know that sun and distance smoothed out contours and turned the deepest gullies and ravines into insignificant smudges of light and shade. Sure enough, as his horse carried him nearer to the awesome barrier, his keen eye picked out the shadows high up on those rock faces that indicated cuts, ledges and overhangs in the apparent smoothness – and when he was within 500 yards of the notch, climbing steadily through a wide canyon that narrowed suddenly not too far ahead of him to lead directly into that forbidding break in the cliffs, he caught a bright flash high up on the sheer wall of rock that was there and gone in an instant and could only have been the reflection of sunlight on metal.

Suddenly, his heart was thumping, his mouth dry even as the cold sweat broke out on his brow. Forcing himself to keep his horse moving up the slope, he guided it with the hard muscles of his thighs and a light touch on the reins and leaned forward to stroke its neck. Under cover of that most natural of movements – and the wide brim of his hat – his eyes were darting, combing the crevices in the rocks above him, searching for the slightest movement, his hands ready to flash in an instant to the stock of the gleaming rifle that nestled so reassuringly beneath his right thigh.

In that manner, using the steepness and severity of the climb to sway his body one way then another so that he was never still in the saddle, he advanced twenty yards, fifty yards – then a hundred yards, and still with nothing to alarm him, nothing to break the heavy silence that lay like a warm and oppressive blanket all around the lonely clatter of his horse's hooves and the increasingly hard rasping of its breathing.

Then, as he moved out of the sunlight and into the cold shadows that marked the entrance to Hole In The Wall, from the heights above him a stone came rattling. It bounced from ledge to ledge, arced high, then clattered on to the trail not ten yards in front of his mount sending gravel flying like buckshot. The horse whinnied, jerked its head wildly and lurched sideways. Caught off balance, Sagger grabbed for the horn with one hand while his other tried in vain to reach the butt of the Winchester '73. But he had been thrown the wrong way. He cursed, used his knees to right the startled animal, let go of the horn and leaned down to his right.

As he did so – as his right hand touched the smooth, polished wood and he began to withdraw the rifle – a mighty blow slammed into his shoulder.

There was no time to react, no time to think, no strength left in his body to do either. He felt himself toppling from the saddle before the crack of the rifle high above him had reached ears that could no longer hear, and fell and went on falling into a blackness that was bottomless and without end.

CHAPTER TWELVE

'A day and a half,' Daniel Sagger said. 'That's how long I've been here in this godforsaken hole. Most of it's been spent sleeping, smoking, lazing around in the sun or watching you and your partners do the same – and I still don't know what the hell's going on. Why did you bring me here, Cajun? More to the point, why are you keepin' on with this crazy law-breaking when it's obvious you're a sick man?'

'Not sick,' Cajun Pride said. 'If it's that obvious, Daniel, then you'll know you're lookin' at a dying man.'

'Every damn one of us is going sooner or later,' Sagger said, and looked critically at Cajun Pride. 'So, tell me, how close are you?'

'Months. Weeks?' Pride shrugged. 'I won't see this year out.'

He was standing outside the cabin in the warm sun, looking off across the valley towards the eastern ridge. Sagger, behind him in the doorway, was aware that his words were harsh, probably painful – Lordy, the man in front of him was nothing more than skin and bone, resplendent in his freshly washed yellow shirt and rakish black hat but a shadow of the gunman Sagger had ridden with when blood ran hot in their young veins and the quest for excitement was an unquenchable thirst. But that was a long time ago and he'd been dragged most of the way to Hole In The Wall by a filthy scoundrel who'd murdered his wife in cold blood – ridden the rest of the way out of a burning curiosity that was still unsatisfied. And just like the man in front of him – but for different though no less important reasons – time was not on his side: he was still convinced that Will would come after him and, with precious hours passing in monotonous inactivity, he knew that before long all hell would break loose.

'Where are O'Brien and Weiss?'

'There's a cabin deeper in the Hole, up the slope a ways.' Pride turned to Sagger, an enigmatic smile on his thin face. 'They've been up there since before dawn. When they get back, you'll get your news.'

Sagger studied the thin man's face, looked deep into his eyes. 'I heard riders in the night. Three, maybe four men. I think they rode straight on by, but I can't be sure. Was that something to do with you? Are they gunmen you've brought in, up there now at that cabin?'

'Maybe.'

'I don't think maybe's good enough, Cajun. The day I rode in I told you what happened to my wife, how one of your men slit her throat and left her in a pool of blood for my kids to find. He's paid for what he did, I told you that, too, but I was wasting my breath because it was like talking to one of those logs.' He jerked a thumb at the cabin wall as Pride turned to face him.

'And I told you I was sorry, but that terrible tragedy had nothing to do with me—'

'So it was Amos Skillin's idea to come after me?'

'No, but—'

'Whose, then? O'Brien's, Weiss's?'

'Leave it be, Daniel.'

'Leave it be?' Sagger laughed harshly. 'Maybe that ain't such a bad idea, Mister Cajun Pride because, by Christ, I'm racked by the grief of what you've done to my family and I've seen nothing here to impress me.'

'That's because here's not where it's going to happen,' Pride said. He sank down on to a rickety stool up against the cabin's resiny log walls, squinted up at his old partner. 'I told you, I'm sorry about your wife, I feel your pain like it was mine – and, Jesus, there's enough of that. But don't you see, what happened to her, the effect it's sure to have on your kids, makes what we're going to do in the next few days all the more important?'

'Nothing,' Sagger said, 'can bring her back.'

'But there's something waiting out there on those plains can make the pain a whole lot easier for you and your family to bear, my friend,' Pride said.

'Out there?' Sagger moved past Pride, slid his back down the cabin wall close to the window until he was hunkered down, then reached into his shirt pocket for the makings. 'Now what,' he said softly, 'could be out there that would interest me?' And without looking at Pride he began rolling a cigarette – and patiently waited.

'A whole heap of cash, that's what,' Pride said after a while, and there was a tremor in his voice.

With a faint, harsh, scraping sound, Sagger dragged the match-head across the sole of his boot, applied the bright flame to the cigarette and inhaled deeply.

'There's no big towns close,' he said, the words pushing out a cloud of smoke, 'and in any case I can't see even you trying to take one of those modern banks with their fancy safes. The stage? – Hell, they stopped using them to move worthwhile amounts of cash years ago.' He glanced sideways at Pride, saw him with his eyes squeezed shut as he fumbled in a pocket of his black vest then delicately drank from the metal flask.

'What's that?'

'Laudanum.' The thin man's voice was tight.

Sagger nodded, looked away and off into the distance with a hollow feeling in his stomach. 'One last throw of the dice,' he said, and lowered his gaze to study the end of his cigarette. 'What is it, Cajun? The cancer?'

But Pride was tucking the flask into his hip pocket and looking up the slope. He came off the stool, stretched, yawned and, as he did so, Sagger caught the sound of hoofbeats and knew the night riders were coming down from the cabin.

Then, even above the rattle of hooves on hard ground, the crack of a shot came rippling through the warm air. As the sharp sound reached them and echoed away up the barren valley that was Hole In The Wall, Cajun Pride swung around with apprehension and something that might have been suspicion in his eyes as he looked at Daniel Sagger.

'Smithy's waving to us,' O'Brien said. He'd gone into the cabin for the field-glasses and had them trained on the rocks high above the distant notch.

'One shot, that's all,' Pride said with emphasis.

Weiss chuckled, and stroked his beard. 'I guess the lawman who figured he was comin' in ain't gonna make it,' he said.

Four horses were tied to the short hitch rail alongside the cabin, a fifth had its reins looped around the branch of a stunted tree on the stony slope. The three men who had ridden down the hill with O'Brien and Weiss were squinting off into the distance, and Sagger reckoned he'd never seen a rougher, sorrier-looking bunch.

But they were the least of his worries. The hollow ache of sadness that had stabbed at the pit of his stomach when he saw Pride using a flask to drown the sudden flare of pain was still there, but it was now overpowered by an uncomfortable itch between his shoulderblades that he hadn't experienced for years. Scratching would do no good, even if he could reach: the itch was a warning that had more than once saved his life during his years riding on the wrong side of the law. He was astounded that it had returned almost as soon as he took the fatal step over that thin line between good and evil – and he knew it was telling him the single shot that had split the morning stillness was the one he had been fearing.

Swiftly, he looked across at O'Brien. The glasses were still clamped to the big man's eyes. Then he grunted, took them down.

'That's it, I guess. Smithy's settled, everything back to normal.'

'Maybe,' Sagger said, 'I should go take a look.'

'No sweat, Daniel,' Pride said. 'All taken care of.'

'Give me something to do after settin' around for so long.' Sagger kept his voice casual, immediately began to walk towards the small corral out back were the other horses lazed. 'I'll send Smithy down for coffee, spell him for a couple of hours.'

'All right, you do that,' Pride said. 'A couple of hours . . . give me time to talk to these fellers. . . .'

'Who the hell're you?'

The snapped words stopped Sagger. He looked back at the sullen man with ice-blue eyes and the lithe, lazy movements of a cat who had led the newcomers down the hill. His companions held back, watching him, and Sagger guessed he was the leader, the man with the fast gun, the ice-cold heart to match his bleak eyes.

'The man I was telling you about,' Pride said, and Sagger realized his old partner knew this dangerous man, had probably ridden with him, stood alongside him as they used their pistols to kill – maybe stepped outside to talk to him last night when Sagger was half asleep. 'This is "Cold Hand" Sagger, Harry. Daniel, shake hands with Harry Tracy.'

Sagger nodded, but curled his lip at the invitation. 'From his manner, I'd say you didn't tell him enough, Cajun,' he said, and casting a look of thinly veiled contempt at the blue-eyed gunslinger, he continued towards the corral.

The terrible nagging itch between his shoulders persisted, strengthened. He knew the lean gunslinger's cold eyes were boring into his back; knew the distant rifle shot had aroused suspicion in the pain-dulled mind of Cajun Pride and that the merest flick of his hand – however repugnant to him that act might be – would signal the end for his old partner, Daniel Sagger. So when Daniel walked away he was listening for the quiet word of command followed by the soft hiss of metal on leather, the click of a hammer cocking, the rattle of boots as men hurriedly stepped out of the line of fire – but heard nothing. Then a murmur of conversation broke out. Behind him, stones did rattle under hard leather, but the feet were moving without haste. By the time he had saddled his horse and turned it towards the distant notch, the cabin door was closed, the flat ground outside the cabin deserted.

Sagger rode hard, pushing down the slope and following the meandering line of the stony creek towards the notch. It took him no more than fifteen minutes to get there, another five to bring the man called Smithy down from his ledge and convince him he was relieved and could go back to the cabin.

'Keep your eyes skinned,' Smithy said, stepping up into the saddle. 'One man rode up, got hisself plugged, but I think I saw a couple more watching him from a half-mile or so back.'

Then, remembering O'Brien and his liking for

field-glasses, as the man rode away Sagger yelled after him, 'If O'Brien can't see me and gets the wind up, tell him so's I can watch those *hombres* out there I've moved to a better position with more cover.' He waved vaguely at the high cliffs as the man looked back, added, 'See you back here in a couple of hours,' received a nod of acknowledgement and watched the grateful lookout point his horse towards the distant cabin and the thought of hot coffee.

'Goddamn!' Jake Cree said.

They'd barely made it to the thin line of stunted trees and tethered their horses when Slim Gillo's sharp eyes caught the puff of white smoke high on the cliffs. Instantly, he grabbed Cree's sleeve and both men snapped their eyes to the distant mounted figure pushing up the steep defile towards the notch leading into Hole In The Wall.

The sound of the shot was the faintest of cracks – yet it filled the watchers with horror.

'He's winged,' Cree said, in a strangled voice.

'But still in the saddle,' Gillo said, squinting. 'Looked like he'd bite the dust, but he's hangin' on, and with enough sense to hightail out of there.'

'Your eyes are younger than mine – but if Will's turned around like you say, he's risking a shot in the back.'

'No. That lookout's up there to issue blunt warnings. If the intruder get's the message and turns back, his job's done.'

'But what about ours?' Cree said. 'This is one hell of a mess, Slim. We're still pinned down outside the

Hole, no nearer to finding Daniel Sagger and now his son's carrying a slug.' He shook his head. 'I blame myself, we should've—'

'I know!' Gillo's jaw was tight with tension. 'As a lawman, you think I ain't aware of what we should've done? But that's over, Will figured the responsibility was his and took off on his own, and we let him go. So now we put things right.'

'If it's not too damn late.'

Gillo's smile was bleak as he kept his eyes pinned on the returning rider. 'He's upright, Jake. I reckon the shock of that bullet knocked him sideways, but if he can recover that fast he can't be too bad hit.'

'Jesus!' Jake Cree said, bitterly directing the curse at his own stupidity and helplessness. 'I'm twice your age and half as wise. Better if I'd stayed behind with Cath and Becky, you had Dave Lee Nelson riding with you.'

'Your time'll come, old man,' Gillo said with dry humour.

And then he said, softly, but with a tautness that grabbed Jake Cree's attention and sent his hand leaping instinctively but futilely to his six-gun, 'There's a rider comin' down from the notch.'

'The hell there is! I thought you said that lookout was dealing out warnings?'

'I've been wrong more than once in my illustrious career,' Gillo said. 'Besides, he ain't chasing too hard after Will and there's something about him that's got me wondering. . . .'

His voice trailed away. Cree watched the gangling lawman ease his six-gun in its holster and step through the gnarled trees to meet Will Sagger and realized he had seriously understimated Cliff McClure's deputy. His lean and lazy demeanour hid a razor-sharp mind, and he was meeting this sudden setback with quick thinking made all the more impressive by his calm assurance.

Deliberately emulating that excellent example, Cree moved with a slow, measured gait through the trees and watched Gillo walk to Will Sagger's horse and help the young rider down out of the saddle. He seemed OK, able to walk, dazed but tossing Cree a weak grin. And beyond him, closer now so that Cree's eyes could see him more clearly, the second rider was coming fast across the grassland.

'You know who that is?' he said, as Will Sagger limped towards him with his hand tight on Gillo's shoulder.

'Knew it all along,' Gillo said, answering for the white-faced Sagger. 'I've watched Daniel Sagger ride into town so many times I'd recognize him six mile off in a real bad mist.'

'Pa?' Will turned on shaky legs, wobbled, clung on to Gillo. 'Hell, you mean all that was wasted effort?'

'For the answer to that, and how the hell your pa got in and out of that hell hole so easy,' Cree said, 'we'll have to wait a while longer – but what about you, son, how bad is it?'

'I'm fine.' Gillo had walked over to the tethered horses and was digging into his saddle-bag. On the level ground below the trees Will Sagger sank down on to the grass, put a hand gingerly to the wet blood soaking through his shirt at the left shoulder. 'I caught a ricochet, came howling off a rock, by the time it reached me it was a hunk of metal no more bothersome than a tired old hornet.'

'You say,' Cree said, 'but I know how you feisty youngsters like to brag. Let Slim have a look at it, patch you up. . . .'

But he was listening to the thud of approaching hooves as his words tailed off, walking back up the slope to the trees and through them into the sunlight, only vaguely aware of what was happening behind him as Gillo returned from his horse with a spare shirt, the sharp ripping sound as he tore it into strips.

Then he was watching the lean figure of Daniel Sagger swing down from the saddle with reckless haste, a look on his face that was apprehension laced with a strong measure of fear reflected in clear grey eyes that brushed across Cree then raked swiftly beyond him to the slope on the far side of the trees.

'Your boy's in good shape, Daniel,' Cree said, and stepped in front of his old friend. 'He caught a rico-chet, and Slim Gillo's about to strap his shoulder.' He reached out to shake hands, the gesture made delib-erately to slow the man down, to reassure him. 'He'll be fine, you can count on it.'

Sagger took his hand almost absently, released it quickly, then made to walk on by. Cree stopped him with his arm.

'Wait a while,' he said, looking into Sagger's eyes. 'There's no rush, Daniel. The last time I saw you – hell, the last several times – you were lookin' at me kind of bleary-eyed over an empty whiskey bottle.

Now this, you ridin' in and out of a nest of rattlesnakes like it's home sweet home, your boy picking up a slug in his haste to track you down. So before we go down and talk to him, would you mind telling an old friend what the hell's been going on?'

'It's something you should all hear,' Daniel Sagger said, and firmly moved Jake Cree out of his path. 'And as I've got less than two hours to do the telling, I think we'd better get on down there.'

CHAPTER THIRTEEN

The small fire was smokeless, clear flames crackling in a hearth of white rocks gathered in the hollow beneath the trees. Along with the smell of the burning mesquite logs there was the rich odour of fresh coffee, and the hot sun and the low murmur of voices added to the atmosphere of lazy tranquillity.

But the peaceful aura masked tension that was like the precursor of an imminent, violent storm and, his back against the rough bark of a stunted tree, Will Sagger sat with knees drawn up a few yards away from the main group, listened without seeming to, awkwardly massaged the gleaming Winchester '73 with a soft cloth as he nursed his wounded shoulder and drew his own conclusions.

The meeting between Will and his pa had been unbearably painful, an emotional coming together after a shared tragedy with fumbling explanations from the older man that offered few surprises, followed by apologies that were swept aside by a son who showed deep if silent satisfaction when he learnt of the death of Amos Skillin.

They had embraced while Jake Cree started the coffee brewing, talked brokenly but with gradually strengthening voices about what had transpired since the flight from Circle C until, with a spoon clattered loudly against tin cups, the gunsmith and the deputy had called them over. And those mundane tasks that brought immense comfort through familiarity – the gurgle and splash of water, the rattle of the pot, the hiss of flames – had been done by compassionate men working with cool efficiency but a deal of haste, for right from the start it had been impressed on them by Daniel Sagger that he had but two hours.

And now, with time running out like sand through a holed bucket, it was much less.

'. . . is that he wants me in with him, and I don't know how to walk away from a man expressing a dying wish.'

Daniel Sagger talking, the words cutting through Will's musing, his pa expressing sentiments that seemed outrageous to a young man brought up by his dead mother to respect Christian values and the law of the land, yet spoken with genuine indecision by the man he now knew to have been the Utah Kid's sidekick.

'It's the business he wants you involved in that gives you your answer,' Jake Cree said, poking thoughtfully at the fire. 'Hell, Daniel, the man's organized the murder of your wife to suck you into pullin' off a train robbery.'

'No,' Sagger said, 'I truly believe he was not behind that.'

From his position against the trees, Will said, 'He knew the calibre of the men he was sending after you. Amos Skillin was lacking in morals. In the end it was Cajun Pride's responsibility.'

'Son, the man's dying of the cancer. You think that leaves him in his right mind, with clear thinking?'

'Yeah, I do. He knows he wants to go out in a blaze of glory, and he wants to take you down with him.'

'So what you do,' Slim Gillo said, 'is you ride away from this, we go back to Ten Mile Halt, you tell Cliff McClure what you know and he'll get on the telegraph to Union Pacific.'

'I've heard nothing except a heap of cash waitin' to be picked up, so Union Pacific's just a guess. But even if I'm right, if I ride away from here the outlaws'll fade into the hills, put off the robbery until the coast's clear – and in the meantime, Cajun won't let up, he'll send another crazy killer to Circle C.'

'Becky'll come to no harm.' Gillo said. 'This time you'll be prepared – *we'll* be prepared.'

Sagger smiled cynically. 'Maybe you're right. But what if I ride away, and the Utah Kid goes ahead without me.'

'You *care* about those fellers?' Will's tone was caustic.

'Him. Not them.' Sagger looked over at his son. 'Yes, I care.'

'Enough to go along with him?'

He watched his pa ponder that question, brow furrowed, both hands clasping the tin cup, his eyes fixed on the flickering flames. Jake Cree had moved away from the heat of the fire and, hat off, was mopping his brow with a bandanna. Slim Gillo had also walked away, and was prowling up the hill to cast his eyes towards the distant notch.

The air was electric.

'I care enough,' Daniel Sagger said at last, 'to go back there and try my damnedest to persuade Cajun to give up this crazy idea, move out of Hole In The Wall to a pleasant town somewhere and spend his last few months with peace of mind.'

'Can't be done,' Cree said, replacing his hat and rounding on his friend. 'The man's fixated. All he can see is him with his old pard alongside him, that mighty train clanking down the tracks, the flash of pistols in the night and the newspaper headlines with his name up there in bold type.'

'I must try, Jake.'

'Where does that leave me?' Slim Gillo had come back down the slope and was standing with hands on hips, the badge glinting on his vest, a stubborn jut to his jaw. 'I'm in possession of information about the possible theft of large amounts of cash from the Union Pacific Railroad Company.' He let that thought and its implications sink in, then said quietly, 'One of the men likely to be involved in that robbery is settin' right here in front of me.'

Daniel Sagger sighed. 'You'd take me in?'

'As a lawman, do I have a choice?'

'Yeah. Keep your mouth shut, and wait.'

Gillo's face darkened. The hand that was resting on his right hip drifted free, brushed his holster. It seemed that they were an instant away from an ugly incident that could end in another violent death –

and then Jake Cree cut in quickly, 'Daniel put that badly, Slim. What he's saying is he'll make his try to change the Kid's mind, but if he can't do it then he'll come out of the Hole and ride with you to Ten Mile.'

And now a thin smile flickered across Daniel Sagger's face as he looked at Slim Gillo. 'And I guess with choices limited for both of us, we'll have to settle for that.'

Watching them, Will saw Jake Cree's diplomatic interruption defuse the situation. Slim Gillo had visibly relaxed, but his eyes were thoughtful. Will's pa was also thoughtful, but Will knew he was waiting to see which way Gillo would swing, and planning accordingly.

'Fair enough.' Gillo nodded, and hunkered down in the grass. 'But in case something happens and you don't make it out of there, Daniel, let me have some names to give McClure.'

'Cajun Pride you know,' Sagger said. 'There's Fergel O'Brien and Karl Weiss, two more whose names I didn't catch, and a feller called Harry Tracy.'

Gillo grunted. 'Tracy's wanted for murder up in Utah. The others you can't name could be his partner, Dave Lant, and a feller called Swede Johnson.'

'I'll listen for those names,' Sagger said. 'But I want you to leave timing and judgement to me. I've got no details. This robbery's going to happen, but it could be as far away as next month, as close as this week. So no matter what you see or hear, stay back. This is my play. If it comes off. . . .'

He waited for Gillo's reluctant nod, stood up, then waited as the deputy also came to his feet.

'Railroad timetables are something I know about,' he said. 'McClure's always got one pinned to the board in the office—'

'That's right,' Will cut in, remembering. 'Ma went to him a year back when she needed some times for a trip she was making. . . .'

'Yeah, well,' Gillo said, after a moment's hesitation, 'what I'm gettin' at is there ain't all that many runs for me to get too easily confused—'

'For God's sake, get on with it, Slim!' Jake Cree said.

'The point is,' Gillo said, 'I'm pretty damn certain from what I know that if your old pard's after the Union Pacific's Overland Flyer, then he'll do it tonight.'

'Explain,' Cree said.

'I don't know where he'll hit it,' Gillo said, 'but that train comes through tonight and the Utah Kid's forced to move fast. That train's always been Butch Cassidy's favourite target, and there's a rumour—'

'Rumour?'

Gillo glared at Cree. 'One of those fellers out of Hole In The Wall who came to Ten Mile after Daniel stopped off at the saloon, Red Keegan heard him talking. About how Cassidy and Kid Curry were plannin' another such raid. But if that's within spittin' distance of the truth. . . .'

Daniel Sagger nodded slowly. Then, wiping his palms on the side of his pants, he came away from the fire and reached across to shake hands with the deputy. 'Thanks, Slim, that gives me something to work on.' He winked cheerfully at Jake Cree and walked over to Will.

'This won't take long,' he said. 'I'll say it again: you've got my thanks for the manly way you handled yourself, arranged for Becky's care – the way you passed the running of the ranch over to Dave Lee Nelson so you could make this ride.'

'Pa—'

'No, you listen: no matter what I said, I reckon Cajun's planning on a fast move' – he looked across at Gillo and nodded as he said that – 'so it'll be over, one way or another, before you know it – and then we'll ride home and pick up the pieces; maybe start afresh.'

'No need. The best years of my life have been those since you rode into Circle C's yard and stayed home for good,' Will Sagger said, and with a lump in his throat he reached out to meet his father's strong hand-clasp. 'When this is over, I'll be happy to have things run like that – exactly the way they were.'

Jumbled words that made no sense were tussling with each other in Daniel Sagger's head as he rode back across the rock-strewn, fissured grassland. Arguments strong enough to get through to a stubborn and ailing outlaw were composed, then discarded, and always in front of him there was the pale face of Cajun Pride, the Utah Kid, the burning light in his eyes as he spoke passionately of one last ride with his old partner.

What monumental task had he set himself?

How do you change the mind of a man who is dying, a man for whom life and death have lost their meaning? How do you tell him that waiting for death in a rocking chair on some sunlit veranda is preferable to the heady exhilaration of a meticulously planned train robbery; that the blaze of glory will come and go with all the fierceness and transience of summer lightning?

The answers to those questions were as elusive as ever when Sagger rattled into the narrow defile with the awareness of having outstayed his time and, even as he pushed his horse through the infamous notch and caught sight once again of the barren outlaw valley, he knew he was in trouble.

The man called Smithy was back, he had O'Brien's field-glasses looped over his shoulder, and one look at his face told Sagger the man had seen too much.

'Friends of yours?'

Confident. Sitting easy in the saddle, half turned so that his hand could reach his six-gun. On his face a look of contempt.

'Who?'

The outlaw turned his head sideways, spat – and went for his gun.

Sagger had heard of time standing still, of a man watching the whole of his life flash before his eyes in his dying moments. Now he was experiencing it, but instead of seeing flashes of his past life he was watching the present fall apart. Even as his hand stabbed for the butt of his Smith & Wesson and he knew – with the confidence of a man who has been there many times before – that he would beat the other man's draw, he was anticipating the sound of the shot echoing across the valley, dreading the repercussions.

Then his mind cleared. He saw Smithy's lips draw back from his teeth in a snarl of triumph, saw the man's pistol come up halfway; saw his hand suddenly caught and its upward swing halted by the thong holding the field-glasses. And, as panic flared in the outlaw's eyes, Daniel Sagger shot him through the heart and watched him go backwards out of the saddle with the light in his eyes fading, his gun-hand still hopelessly tangled.

The shot seemed to resound like the report of a cannon. Moving fast, Sagger leaped from the saddle, left his horse's reins trailing and ran to the fallen outlaw. Even as he sprang across the intervening distance, his mind was tormented by visions of what his friends might do. Hold back, he thought, for Christ's sake, Slim, when you hear that shot, hold off. Then, the prayer echoing and re-echoing in his brain, he bent to the dead outlaw and heaved and wrestled him up off the ground and across his saddle. The outlaw's wrists and ankles he lashed together under the horse's belly with a rawide thong dug hastily from his saddle-bag. The field-glasses he slung over his own shoulder. Then, breathless, sweat dripping from his chin, he mounted up and set off down the slope at a trot leading the outlaw's horse.

And all the way down from the notch and along the winding creek to the cabin where Cajun Pride and his band of outlaws waited he was searching for the words that would convincingly explain his actions – and he could find not a single one.

CHAPTER
FOURTEEN

Harry Tracy was to the forefront of those awaiting him as Daniel Sagger urged the two horses up the slope and across the stony ground fronting the cabin with the dead outlaw flopping loose and heavy across the saddle. Flanking Tracy, but a step or so back from the cold-eyed outlaw's broad shoulders, were the two men Sagger now assumed to be Dave Lant and the Swede, Johnson.

Behind them and the other men, in the doorway of the cabin with his hands braced against the frame, Cajun Pride was a fragile figure who yet managed to dominate the scene as, with burning gaze, he watched the outlaws gather for Sagger's approach.

Sagger swung down. The man he took to be Lant went over to the outlaw hanging belly down over the horse, took a quick look, glanced back at Tracy.

'Plugged tru der heart, I tink.'

Weird accent. Swedish, so Johnson not Lant.

'And I think your lookout went loco,' Sagger said

easily. Without looking at the man he brushed close to Tracy, went on by and approached Pride. 'I thought I saw something, the flash of sunlight on metal, rode out through the notch and down a ways. I was mistaken. But when I came back in, Smithy was there and would have shot me dead if I hadn't got him first.' He looked straight into Pride's eyes. 'Went loco, or was following orders,' he said. 'Which is it, Cajun?'

'Smithy never came near me,' Pride said, and his gaze drifted over Sagger's shoulder. 'I slept a while, he stayed outside drinking coffee with the others.' His eyes came back to Sagger, and when he spoke again his voice was pitched louder, carrying clearly. 'But you know damn well if I want anybody along with me when we take that train—'

'Nobody said nothing to Smithy.' This was Harry Tracy, walking over to the cabin. 'We smoked, drank java, cracked some jokes. Smithy was glad of the break, when his time was up he went back to relieve Sagger.' His cold blue eyes turned to Sagger. 'This feller's feedin' you a load of horse shit, and I don't want him with us.'

'*You* don't want?' Pride came out of the doorway and stepped sideways to look past Sagger. 'You're here at my invitation, Tracy. You don't like what you see, ride on a ways and talk to Cassidy and Logan, see if they like the way you shape up.'

Tracy grunted. 'You know we don't hit it off—'

'So stay. And welcome. But lay off my partner.'

For a long, tense few seconds it seemed that Tracy was not going to let his suspicions lie – was not going to take orders from a frail man who looked incapable of pulling a six-gun. Then, with a shrug, he turned away. The others were already lifting the dead man down from the horse. Pride called out, 'Take him out back, bury him.' Then he turned to Sagger, jerked his head and went back into the cabin.

The sun sinking in the west turned the interior of the cabin into an abattoir, its low rays cutting through the small window to splash the walls with lurid colour. That ghastly, blood-red light was reflected on to the faces of the two men who sat talking, the mood it created one of grim foreboding. Cajun Pride was moving that night – no, within the hour – and so far, despite racking his brain, an increasingly desperate Daniel Sagger had not come up with one argument likely to disrupt those plans, to change the mind of a dying man intent on writing his name into the history books.

Now, with time running out, he knew that the only recourse left to him was the truth – and he didn't think his old partner was in any mood to listen.

'You think I was square with you when I rode up?'

'I don't care one way or the other, Daniel. You're riding with me, that's all that counts.'

This was Pride's cabin, he had banished the other outlaws from it so that he could prepare without their intrusive presence, and he was moving around the confined space like a man familiar with his surroundings – even, Sagger thought, like a man who was at home and comfortable. And he knew that could easily be true. A person who has been a long

121

time ill will pine for his home, will settle there like a sick dog in its basket, will show a growing reluctance to move outside that dwelling – however humble.

Now, with his Colt six-gun cleaned and oiled and the gunbelt laid out ready to be strapped around his lean waist, he was sitting on the edge of the cabin's only cot and slipping his feet into handsome leather boots.

'Did you ever consider I might have been trailed here?'

'First thing I thought of.'

'And what now?'

Pride looked up, one boot on, his greying hair flopping over his forehead.

'They're out there, whoever they are, you saw them – and Smithy knew it and that's why you killed him.'

'That was in your mind when you let me relieve him.'

'Sure it was. But I figured it'd be two or three men, not a posse, you couldn't risk bringing them into the Hole to come up against the men I've got, those other shootists in the cabin up the hill, listening. . . .'

He lapsed into silence, grunting occasionally as he finished donning his boots, once pausing for some time and taking a draught of laudanum from the flask he carried in his black vest and closing his eyes until the drug sent pain into the background.

At the table, bathed in the light of sunset, watching the men outside saddling up, tightening cinches – the one, the dangerous one, sending brooding glances towards the cabin – Sagger digested what he

122

had been told and wondered where it left him. And at long last he knew it made no difference.

'Give it up, Cajun.'

'Don't be a fool.'

'Die in peace, my friend. In your own bed.'

'This is my bed.' Pride slammed a hand down on the cot, drew a cloud of dust from the thin blankets. 'Would you choose to die here?'

'Then ride with me to Circle C, eat well, en—'

'No!'

Pride reached for his gunbelt, held the holster flat in his left hand, slid the six-gun out and shoved it back hard with a decisive thwack and looked up with a half smile.

'You haven't listened to one word since you rode in here, Daniel—'

'And now you're making the same foolish mistake.'

'Oh, I'd listen,' Pride said, standing somewhat unsteadily and pulling the gunbelt around his waist. 'I'd listen, but nothing you're saying beats anything I've got planned. I'm stopping the Union Pacific close to Casper. I'm doing it tonight, because those fellers up the slope have got the same idea and I intend to get there first. You're riding with me. Those friends of yours can try to stop me. They'll die. I won't be stopped – but if I am stopped, it'll be at a time and place of my choosing, and it'll be with my boots on.'

And punctuating the words with a gesture of finality, he pushed the tongue of the gunbelt through the buckle and snapped it tight.

CHAPTER FIFTEEN

'I guess I should have spoken up,' Will Sagger said, 'but seeing Pa like that, after what happened back at the ranch. . . .'

'We're all in this,' Jake Cree said. 'We heard him say it could be next month, next week – yet nary a one of us thought twice about what that meant, how long we were supposed to sit out here.'

'I've got my opinions, voiced some of them when Daniel was here,' Slim Gillo said, 'but it wasn't the time to go one step further, or decide if my thinking's right or miles off target.'

'Now it is,' Jake Cree said. 'We let a good man ride into danger like he was settin' off to a barn dance – no mention of how he'd get in touch, what signals we should expect; what to do if none came – so you'd best speak out now or we'll still be here at Christmas.'

It was late evening, the shadows long, the embers in the smoke-blackened rocks glowing bright then dark in a shifting pattern of colour before the warm and gentle breeze. All three men were close to the fire and the sweet smell of burning logs, lying in an ungainly sprawl, hunkered awkwardly, rolling yet another cigarette, gazing off into the gathering dusk, poking idly at the embers with a stick – evincing all the restless mannerisms of men who had been too long idle yet were uncertain how to break away. And always, for each of them, there was the looming menace of the high purple cliffs set against the fiery western skies with the notch leading into Hole In The Wall cut into them like the sharp V of a rifle's rear sight.

Nothing had moved.

They had heard no sound.

'What I don't understand,' Dave Lee Nelson said, 'is why Daniel rode under that weird Cold Hand name, and how he kept that and his outlaw past under his hat for so long.'

Nelson, like Will earlier in the day, was sitting away from the fire. He had ridden in on a lathered horse not too long after Daniel Sagger had headed back to the Hole, the badge on his vest glittering in the rays of the westering sun. Quickly, he had off-saddled and brought the men up to date on the happenings back at Ten Mile – eliciting a grin of pride from Cree when he was told of his wife's part in the affair. Nelson mentioned his elevation to deputy marshal with a wary glance at Slim Gillo – who nodded approval – while McClure's swift decision to send Nelson out to intercept the men chasing Daniel Sagger sent an already admired marshal's reputation soaring.

'Cold Hand,' Gillo said, in answer to his question, 'because there never was a man could hold a six shooter steadier than Daniel. How he kept it under his hat? Well, I guess he lost himself in the world of small-time ranching, and when he did that he lost everybody else, too.'

'Until Cajun Pride got sick and ambitious and decided to hunt him down,' Jake Cree said bitterly. For a few moments there was silence as all four of them reflected on what was, and what might have been. Then Cree said, 'You were about to say, Slim?'

'They'll stop the train tonight, I've said that and I'm sure of it,' Slim Gillo said at last, his joints cracking like distant gunfire as he eased closer to the fire. 'That deadline means they're already short of time; they'll be looking at somewhere real close. So, stickin' my neck out, I say they'll hit the Overland Flyer about ten miles after it pulls out of Casper.'

'And stopping it's their first problem,' Jake said, eyes narrowed in thought. 'You reckon what, Slim? A barrier of some kind, a pile of rocks or timber?'

'Lantern,' the deputy said. 'Faster and easier to wave them down with a red light. Ain't a train driver around wouldn't at least slow down out of curiosity – and when he does that, they've got him.'

Watching the two older men, listening to their talk, Will Sagger was gingerly moving his shoulder to prevent it stiffening while finding it difficult to reconcile the father he knew of old with this new man who was at home with a band of outlaws. And despite knowing he had been dragged into it, despite his pa's reassurance that it would be over quickly, Will couldn't rid his mind of the awful conviction that those words had been for his benefit and had hidden Daniel Sagger's deep uncertainty and misgivings.

Cajun Pride, the Utah Kid. Was he likely to walk away from a spectacular train robbery just because a man he had hounded asks him to? Could Daniel Sagger even risk making that request when surrounded by lawless gunslingers eager for the next fast dollar? In Will's opinion, if his pa did manage to put his question to the Utah Kid, it would be treated with disbelief, and brushed aside – hell, in Pride's estimation Will's pa was cut from the same cloth, had gained his reputation as Daniel 'Cold Hand' Sagger, partner and equal of the infamous Utah Kid.

Fame beckoned. Pride could envisage two ageing gunslingers rekindling the flames of youth and going out with an almighty bang. For a dying man, that made some warped kind of sense, but for a man who still had everything to live for . . .

'From what you've told me,' Dave Nelson said, cutting pertinently through Will's thoughts after another lengthy silence, 'there's still an unexplained gunshot, a possibility that Daniel's no longer in the game.' He looked across at Will. 'I guess that's a blunt way of putting it, feller, but it's something we've got to face.'

'Possible, but not likely,' Will said, knowing there was little on which to base such optimism, yet convinced nevertheless that his pa was still alive. 'When they do come riding out of the Hole' – he grinned crookedly – 'this Cold Hand Sagger'll be right there with them.'

'And we'll be right behind,' Jake said, 'ready to pull him out if things get rough.'

'We will,' Slim Gillo said, and Nelson nodded his head in agreement.

'If we know where they're headed,' Jake Cree said, 'if your guess is good and they are planning on hitting the train this side of Casper – then we can stay well back, not risk being spotted.'

'That was no guess,' Gillo said. 'It's a prediction I'll stake my reputation on.'

'You ain't got one to stake,' Cree said, the tension easing for an instant as he grinned, 'but when this night's out that could all change.'

'Deputy leads raid that foils daring train robbery,' Will quoted. 'You'll snatch the headlines off the Utah Kid, Slim, come election time you'll get more votes than Cliff McClure.'

'Shucks,' Gillo said, 'all of a sudden my goddamn hat's too tight.'

And then Will Sagger said softly, but with such intense urgency that his words quickened the pulse of each man around that fire, 'I hear hoofbeats; there's a bunch of riders comin' down from Hole In The Wall.'

The seven men came down from the notch in a rowdy, winding column and hit the flat land at a gallop. Cajun Pride had chosen this grandiose manner of descent as a statement to whoever might be watching that he and his men were unstoppable. And he had insisted that Daniel Sagger ride immediately behind him and, when they were out of the Hole and the pace moderated, come alongside him, partners riding stirrup as they led their men into that final, glorious battle.

Listening to all this, Sagger was of the opinion that his old friend's bodily sickness had mentally unbalanced him, but he had no option other than to comply. And so he was behind Pride when his horse came tumbling down from the pass, drew alongside him as they headed east across the ridged grassland and, in the natural way of a man on the lookout for enemies, let his eyes wander as he rode to pick up any sign of the three men who were awaiting his signal.

There was no sign, and that gave him considerable satisfaction. They were staying back, keeping under cover and, because they had no time to make the ride to Ten Mile Halt to alert the authorities, they would certainly follow the outlaw band.

With those two stalwarts and my own son alongside me, Sagger thought, we'll defeat these bastards. And if he did allow anything to trouble him, it came from his uncomfortable musings on the ultimate fate of Cajun Pride, the Utah Kid.

'Brooding?'

Pride's voice cut through his thoughts and the thunder of racing hoofs.

'Cogitating on what lies ahead. Wondering if you've had second thoughts.'

'If I have,' Pride said, 'they've everything to do with how we conduct this raid, damn all to do with quitting.'

'Then that's your loss, my friend.'

'Loss?' Pride laughed gaily. 'Come on, nobody's a loser in this one, Daniel, and if you ride away from it hating my guts, you'll ride away a rich man.'

'You figured on a foolproof way of doing this?'

'Nothing's foolproof. We use a lantern to halt the train, we board her, we persuade the messenger to give us the money.' He glanced across at Sagger. 'Step at a time, Daniel. You and me, we'll pull it off.'

The two men lapsed into silence. Time passed; as the group pushed on hard the terrain changed to become hillier, and with the sun well down the land was lost in darkness that would only be relieved with the coming of the moon.

Fifteen miles on, the horses blowing, the moon still not in evidence, Pride turned in the saddle, looked back across the following riders and called a halt. They had reached an area of low hills and, to Sagger, it seemed that Pride had chosen his stopping place carefully: they had just taken a right fork, and a high bluff was blocking any view of their back-trail. There, the group came together, milling for a few moments, then settling as the horses dropped their heads to sniff out the available grass. O'Brien fumbled in his pocket, came up with a rolled cigarette, reached for a match.

'Yeah,' Pride said with approval, as the match flared. 'I reckon the more light we show, the more noise we make, then the more natural it looks and sounds.'

O'Brien lit the cigarette, flicked the match away and said, 'How come?'

'We're being followed.'

131

Sagger snapped his head around, saw Pride watching him.

'I heard nothing.'

Pride shrugged. 'I guess a man near death has sharpened senses. They've been with us since the Hole. And now we fix them.'

The cold-eyed killer, Harry Tracy, eased his horse over. 'How many?'

'Four.' Pride shook his head. 'Don't matter anyhow. A small bunch, that I do know.'

'Enough of us here to take them.'

'Except we've got other, more important work to do.' Pride nodded to O'Brien. 'Fergel, when we move off I want you and Karl to remain here. Leave your horses now, take your rifles up on to that bluff. We'll give you time to get settled – ten minutes should do it.'

O'Brien grinned. 'Got it.'

He went to his horse, moved it off the trail and tethered it to a low tree, then slipped his rifle from its boot. While the outlaw stood by waiting for Karl Weiss to do the same, Sagger looked at Cajun Pride, his yellow shirt a beacon in the gloom.

'Why don't I stop behind with them? Could be a posse, and an ambush like that needs a feller with experience—'

Harry Tracy cut him off with a low laugh. 'Experience in what, back-shootin'? Hell, there's only one reason you want to stay behind and that's to stop O'Brien and Weiss and warn your friends.'

'Is that right, Daniel?'

'I gave you my reason.' Sagger turned away from

Pride, watched O'Brien and Weiss leave their horses and fade away into the darkness and shook his head. 'Please yourself. I don't know who's following us – or even if there is anyone back there – but if you're banking on hardbitten riders being stopped by a couple of greenhorns. . . .'

Feigning utter disgust he went across to his horse, made a great show of checking its rig. Short of walking out on Cajun Pride and showing his hand, there was nothing more he could do to help Will, Cree and Gillo. Three men. Yet Pride had said four, and he was rarely wrong. For a moment Sagger pondered on the identity of the fourth rider, then pushed him into the background. It didn't matter. Three or four, their only hope was to stay wide awake, be constantly aware that discovery was always likely, ride with their eyes skinned for a possible ambush. And, even as the thoughts raced through his mind, Sagger's confidence received a boost as the rising moon drifted from behind low clouds. All right, that might help the two drygulchers – but Gillo was a good deputy carrying with him the wisdom of Cliff McClure and, if he'd taken charge and kept the others in the shadows, the two on top of the bluff would be exposed and who could predict the outcome?

The only certainty was that Sagger needed them. He could ride along with Cajun Pride, keep hammering away at him, weakening his resolve; trying to convince him that the right way to everlasting peace of mind was the law-abiding way; but if came down to one man stopping a train robbery when up against the likes of Tracy, Johnson and Lant – well, he'd been out of the game for far too long.

'That's it, time's up,' Pride said. 'Let's move on out.'

With a jingle of bridles, the soft snorts of the horses and the squeak of leather, the five remaining riders pulled away and, moving stealthily across the lusher grass up against the slopes, they slipped away into the darkness.

'Still talking, I guess,' Nelson said.

They'd almost stumbled on the resting outlaws; would have done so but for Slim Gillo's insistence that periodically they should rein in, keep perfectly still – and listen.

That listening had paid off. In the hilly country they had entered, sound didn't carry well, and the faint whispers that reached them were almost drowned by the drumming of their horses' hooves reflected back from the steep slopes. But they'd stopped in time, pulled back. Now they were a quarter-mile on the other side of a high bluff, the men standing as they rested their horses off the trail, watched the thin moon rise, and waited.

'How much further?'

Gillo looked at Cree. 'Ten miles. An hour's riding?'

'And the train comes through when?'

'Christ, leave that to them,' Gillo said. 'All we do is tag along, figure out how to get between them and the Overland Flyer.'

'Only one way,' Nelson said, 'and it ain't easy.' He

rubbed his horse's neck absently, said, 'Anybody count those fellers as they came down from the Hole?'

'Seven,' Will said. He had squinted into the sun's waning light from the shelter of the stunted trees, watching the descent from Hole In The Wall with the gleaming Winchester in the crook of his arm. The outlaws had come tumbling fast and raucously from their lair in single file, then pulled a plume of dust across the grassland as they rode by in a rough arrowhead formation with two men at the front.

'Pa was there,' he said, 'alongside a feller in a yellow shirt, black hat.'

'That'd be Cajun Pride,' Slim Gillo said. 'His manner of dressing was on his dodger. Always did like to make himself the centre of attention, so this valedictory fling with his old pard along to cast admiring glances at him should've been expected.'

'Valedictory,' Jake Cree said, and shook his head.

'An educated lawman,' Dave Lee Nelson said.

'Horseshit,' Slim Gillo said, and spat into the grass.

'They're moving!'

Even as he snapped the words Will, at great risk to his wounded shoulder, had run to his horse and was leaping recklessly into the saddle. The others paused for a moment to listen. Clearly, from the other side of the bluff, hoofbeats could be heard rattling away into the distance. Tripping over their own feet, they rushed to follow Will's lead, flung themselves into the saddle and spurred out on to the trail.

Gangling Slim Gillo had the fastest horse. Perhaps,

also, Will thought as they raced towards the bluff, he was keen to confirm his position as senior lawman, put Dave Lee Nelson in his place. Certainly he swiftly hit the front, whipping the loose ends of his reins back and forth in front of him as he urged his straining mount to greater speed.

Those reins were still lashing from side to side when the horse's legs went from under it and Slim went flying from the saddle to bite the dust. The crack of the rifle that had downed the deputy was followed by a second. Will grunted, hearing the dull thump, sensing the terrible shock of the bullet. His horse jerked under him, threw its head high and went down, sliding gallantly on haunches and stiff forelegs before buckling and rolling limply sideways as Will leaped clear.

His eyes, screwed up against the settling dust and the pain of his jarred shoulder, were everywhere as he rolled. Slim was flat on his face, as still as a felled tree. Jake and Dave Lee Nelson had been taking up the rear; when the shots came they had swung hard off the trail. Now bright muzzle flashes lit up the night like summer lightning as they blazed away at the bluff.

Wincing, Will staggered to his feet and ran to join them. He dropped to his knees alongside Cree, said, 'You got them spotted?'

'Saw the flashes clear as day. Damn fools are together – and I think Dave got one.'

'If they're fools,' Will said, 'what does that make us?'

'Double damned for stupidity,' Dave Lee Nelson

said scathingly. 'Listen, you two lay down covering fire, I'm going up the hill.'

'Listen to the man,' Cree said, flashing Will a grin. 'Off you go then, Deputy – but take care!'

The moon was drifting in and out of the high clouds. Brush crackled as Nelson drifted away into the gloom. Will drew his six-gun and, with Cree matching him bullet for bullet, began drilling measured shots into the crown of the bluff.

'Slim?' Cree said through his teeth.

'Down, not moving.'

'You hurt?'

'No more than I was – but Pa's rifle's out there . . .'

Cree chuckled drily. 'You realize we're playin' that same damn fool game, settin' so close together one shot could kill the both of us?'

'I guess you've forgotten everything you were taught when you were Johnny Reb fighting for the glory of the South,' Will said – then ducked instinctively as a volley of shots rang out from high above.

'Hold your fire,' Cree said, and tilted his six-gun. 'He's in amongst them.'

'I'll get Pa's rifle, check on Slim.'

'No—'

But Will was not listening. Pouching his six-gun, conscious that the crackle of gunfire up above had ceased, he ran to his downed horse, dragged the Winchester from its boot then raced to where Slim Gillo had fallen.

He was no longer there, and his horse had climbed to its feet and was standing at the far side of the trail.

The moon slid from behind a cloud, revealing scuff marks in the dust. They led to the side of the trail, and when Will followed them he found the lanky deputy sitting up against a boulder, long legs stretched out in front of him as he clamped a rolled bandanna against the spreading wet stain under his arm, and cursed under his breath.

'Bad?'

'Flesh wound, in and out, but I'm bleeding like a stuck pig.'

Brave words spoken by a man whose tight voice betrayed his agony. Will reached out, grasped his shoulder encouragingly, then turned as, thirty feet away, Nelson came crashing out of the brush.

'Come on.'

With difficulty he got Gillo on to his feet and walked him to where Cree was now standing talking to Nelson. There, Gillo sank down again with a groan.

'He got them both,' Cree said, nodding at Nelson. 'We can ride, I guess – but we're down one man and two horses.'

'No,' Will said, 'it's just the man. Slim's horse is OK, and those two fellers must have left theirs somewhere around . . .'

He wandered back to the trail as Jake Cree crouched to tend to the wounded deputy and Nelson went for their horses. Slim's horse trotted out of the gloom towards Will; over where the trail had been cut up by the fall, he found Slim's six-gun; and, with a slap on the rump that sent Slim's horse trotting to join the others, he manhandled the saddle off his own dead horse and toted it on to the grass.

'Slim reckons he'll be happy where he is,' Cree said.

'Happy!' Slim said, with an attempt at a sickly grin. 'Do I have a choice?'

'One of us could stay behind,' Nelson said, 'but we're up against tough odds.'

'I told you,' Slim said. 'Go get the job done.'

'Two down. That leaves five,' Jake Cree said.

'And one of those is ours,' Will said.

'Yeah,' Slim said tightly, 'but the four left to deal with will be the best – Harry Tracy, Johnson, Dave Lant.'

'And Cajun Pride,' Cree said, 'a man already dying, and intent on going out in a blaze of glory.'

'Well,' Dave Lee Nelson said, 'if that's what the man wants, what the hell are we waiting for?'

'Damn right,' Will Sagger said. He dragged Slim's rifle out of its boot and handed it to the deputy, replaced it with his pa's Winchester, and once again he was first into the saddle as they mounted up, pulled out on to the trail and rode into the night in search of a locomotive's haunting whistle.

CHAPTER SIXTEEN

The railway lines were twin ribbons of iron arrowing across the grassland, their smooth upper surfaces glittering in the fitful moonlight and already singing like twin tuning forks under the immense weight and power of the Overland Flyer.

For the train was close now, very close – and even Daniel Sagger, who wanted no part of this robbery, was caught up in the excitement. Dave Lant had walked down the slope to place a red lantern on a sleeper in the centre of the tracks. Now, hopping like a jack-rabbit over rough grass tussocks, he hot-footed it back to where outlaws and horses were gathered behind a small stand of trees.

'You see how easy it is?' Cajun Pride said slyly, cajolingly. 'Stick with me, Cold Hand, see this through, and you'll be a rich man. Hell, I'll even leave my share to you in my will, in six months or less you'll be double rich – so how does that sound?'

'It sounds like there's still time to call it off,' Sagger said, allowing the rising tide of excitement to carry him along but tempering it with righteousness and giving it direction and force. 'Turn your back on this madness, ride away with me now, Cajun, or—'

'Or what?'

That was Harry Tracy, belligerent, jaw jutting, blue eyes as cold as the hard metal of those vibrating railway lines.

'Was I talking to you?' Sagger said curtly, his eyes still on Pride.

Tracy stepped close, thrust out a stiff arm and slammed the heel of his hand into Sagger's shoulder, rocking him backwards.

'No, but I'm talking to you, and what I'm asking is, Utah rides with you – or what?'

'Forget it, Harry,' Cajun Pride said, swiftly stepping across to put a restraining hand on Tracy's shoulder as he slid his wasting frame between the two men. 'We've got work to do, and time's running out.'

'Yah, I tink we have a train to rob,' Johnson said, as Tracy shook off Pride's hand and continued to glare at Sagger. 'Why the hell you argue?'

But Tracy was not to be put off, and the Swede's words had given him fresh ammunition.

'How do we rob a train,' he said, 'when we've got a smart aleck amongst us dead set on pulling out the man who thought up the whole idea?'

'That train's getting close, Harry,' Dave Lant warned breathlessly. He was away from the group,

142

and after a glance back at the red lantern he was lookin east along the tracks. Sagger pointedly ignored Tracy, followed Lant's gaze and thought he detected a glow in the distance that could have come from the Flyer's smoke stack.

'Settle down,' Cajun Pride said, 'for Christ's sake and for the sake of this robbery—'

'Hell, Utah, can't you see it?' Harry Tracy said. 'The partner you dragged into this, he's gonna get us all killed, he—'

'Enough!'

Slight, pale, a man with greying hair and a voice that could slip from strength to weakness in one painful moment, Cajun Pride was still a potent force. He had placed himself as a barrier between Sagger and Tracy, and now his voice cracked like a whip as he whirled to face Harry Tracy.

'I pulled Daniel in because we rode together in the past, and we'll ride together tonight. If you don't like that. . . .'

'I like it fine,' Tracy said, scowling, 'but I can't say the same for Sagger. So ask him. Is he going along with this, is he going to pull his weight? – because if he ain't, then I want him to get the hell out of here.'

'Daniel?'

Sagger hesitated. The train was a hammering presence hurtling down on the waiting owlhoots, excitement and urgency were palpable forces ripping a man's common sense to tatters – yet when he fought that excitement, overcame it and obeyed those instincts that screamed at him to turn his attention to the west, to listen for approaching hoofbeats – he heard nothing. He had no way of knowing if Will, Cree and Gillo had come through the ambush; no way of knowing if they were even now out there in the darkness, listening, waiting. . . .

And suddenly the four watching outlaws were jumpy, anxious to get the bad-tempered dispute settled because now there could be no doubt: the glow to the east had brightened, sparks could be seen drifting like fireflies against the night sky and, even as they all became aware of a strengthening rumble that could be felt and heard but could not be ignored, a mournful whistle cut through the tense silence and softly, with awe in his voice, Dave Lant said, 'Jesus Christ, just listen to her come!'

Lant was carrying the dynamite in his saddle-bags. Sagger knew that if the train stopped, the outlaws would be on it, hammering on the express car's doors, blowing them apart if the messenger refused to open up, piling in and doing the same to the iron safe if they got another refusal.

Violence. Bloodshed. Good men dying.

Without his friends, he was a man alone and powerless. But if he allowed the robbery to proceed – and, dear Lord, what alternative did he have? – then he would have the backing of other men, those stalwarts on the train who would violently repel the outlaws if the chance came their way. And, Sagger thought, if he stayed at the back of the band then the outlaws would be caught in the jaws of a pincer and . . .

They were waiting. Hard eyes stared at him. Tracy's hand was close to his six-gun and Swede Johnson, influenced by the cold-eyed killer's naked aggression, had moved to the side to give himself a clear view and was also ready for gunplay. Suspicion was like a bad smell, a bad taste, and Sagger knew that if he didn't answer quickly . . .

'Goddammit, Daniel,' Pride growled.

'Get to it,' Sagger said. 'I'm with you.'

With a sudden rush that could only have come from relief Pride turned to him, wrapped him in a surprisingly strong embrace, then stepped back with his hands still on Sagger's shoulders.

'You'll never regret it,' he said, eyes burning in the darkness. 'And I'm not talking about money, I'm talking about what this means to me, and how you'll see it in the years to come.'

And then he wheeled away and it was all action.

For the daring robbery that would bring his career to a dazzling, climactic close, Cajun Pride had chosen the start of a straight coming out of a tight curve, reasoning that if the engineer had reduced the Flyer's speed for the bend he would more easily pick out the warning lantern's red glow as he hit the straight, more easily react before the train picked up speed.

Everything was going according to plan.

The Overland Flyer's lantern became visible, like the staring eye of some huge animal racing along on the other side of the trees lining the start of the long bend. The roar of the big locomotive pulsed, then hammered at sensitive ears. The very earth shook beneath their feet.

Then the roar diminished: the train was slowing.

'Easy now,' Cajun Pride said.

Closer, closer, slowing all the time as the bend tightened. And now, at the rear of the long, dark bulk that was the huge locomotive, they could see the glow from the footplate and, outlined against it, a shadowy figure leaning out to watch the way ahead. Out from the fringe of trees the Flyer sped, the rails straightening before it, the long straight beckoning – and then, abruptly, the squeal of brake blocks, the hiss of steam as the engineer hauled back on the throttle; the screech of iron wheels sliding on the iron track and the stink of hot metal—

'Not yet.'

Cajun Pride screamed the warning as the outlaws leaped forward and swung into the saddle. Faces white in the thin moonlight, they eased towards the edge of the trees, but waited there, reins tight as they held back the excited horses and watched the train slow, slow. . . .

'All right, now, let's go!'

And with with one final glance behind him, Daniel Sagger touched his horse with his heels and took it at an easy pace after the outlaws who were plunging down the slope towards the glittering tracks and the Union Pacific's Overland Flyer which, within feet of the smoking red lantern, was drawing to a grinding halt.

CHAPTER
SEVENTEEN

Will Sagger witnessed the outlaws' charge from the crest of a rise 500 yards to the east, reining in Slim Gillow's dancing horse and squinting across the moonlit landscape to a dark stand of trees and, beyond that, a pinprick of red light standing between the rails in front of a huge locomotive almost lost in billowing clouds of white steam. And, even as he watched, the crackle of gunfire drifted to them and they could see muzzle-flashes reflected in the windows of the stationary train.

'I count five,' Jake Cree said, 'so your pa's riding with them.'

'He'll have his reasons.'

'Hell,' Cree said, 'on his own against those varmints there's damn all else he *can* do.'

'So what are we waiting for?' Dave Lee Nelson said, and without lingering for their reply he put spurs to his horse and set off across the intervening distance at full gallop.

The scene they were bearing down on was like something from Dante's Inferno, smoke and flame and dark, milling figures, and the raucous cries of violent men going about their deadly work.

Will and Jake Cree caught up with Nelson and rode with him. As they drew near to the train, Will thought he could see his father, several yards up slope from the group and apparently doing nothing to help or hinder – but his attention was swiftly drawn to the footplate where two men were locked in a violent struggle against the glow of the locomotive's furnace.

'They get the engineer off there,' Cree said, 'that train's not going anywhere in a hurry.'

And with a glance at the little gunsmith, hat-brim flattened by the breeze, his eyes blazing with excitement, Will drew his six-gun and sent three fast shots winging low over the top of the locomotive.

As the shots whistled overhead, faces turned towards them. The night rang with cries of confusion and anger. On the footplate, the two men broke apart and, taking advantage of the distraction, the engineer loosed a violent, swinging kick and sent his adversary crashing backwards to the ground.

'That's tossed the fox in with the chickens,' Nelson said, flashing Will a savage grin.

Then they were closing fast on the outlaw band, and all was pandemonium.

The man who had fallen from the footplate took one look at the advancing riders and ran, limping, for his horse. Those who had raced towards the express car were caught in two minds, finally decided that flight was the only option and turned back to the horses. One man tripped and went down in a heap, and Will saw a sack fall and sticks of dynamite spill out into the wet grass.

'Move out!' Will roared, and flapped a hand wildly at the engineer. He caught the man's wave of acknowledgement, heard the almost instant hiss of steam and the slamming of a metal brake lever, and the train began to inch forward. The red lamp went over with a crackle of broken glass. When it winked out, the outlaws seemed to lose all heart.

Still rushing towards the disorganized band, Will ducked in the saddle as a slug buzzed angrily past his ear. But it was a wild shot. The outlaws were falling over themselves in the rush for their horses, casting hasty glances over their shoulder as they scrambled into the saddle, then wheeling away and snapping shots that did nothing more than punch holes in the night sky.

One stayed behind. Instead of joining the frantic flight, this man rode fast up the slope to where Daniel Sagger sat his horse, watching. And as he rode, Will saw the flash of a six-gun, roared, 'Pa, look out now!' and was sickened to see the man pull alongside Daniel Sagger and reach across to point the six-gun's muzzle at his head.

'Stay back!' he yelled. 'Come any closer, and he gets it.'

'This is when we need Slim to throw names at us,' Jake said. 'But even without him, I'd say that's Cajun Pride, the Utah Kid.'

'And we've got a stand-off,' Will said.

'What do you hope to gain?' Dave Lee Nelson shouted, above the rattle of the departing Flyer.

'Time. Another chance at the Overnight Flyer when you ain't around.'

'Your time's running out,' Will said, pulling alongside Nelson and Cree as they drew rein. 'From what I hear, you're a dead man refusing to lie down.'

'Jesus!' Jake Cree breathed. 'I'll bet that one hurt.'

Undeterred, Will said, 'Leave my pa to get on with his life—'

'It's all right.' They saw Daniel Sagger lift a hand, push the six-gun away from his head and watch the Utah Kid slip it into its holster. He said, 'I set out for Hole In The Wall to talk to Cajun. I'll continue to do that in the time he's got left. For an old friend that's maybe the least I can do.' His face was pale in the wan moonlight. His last words seemed to hang in the air, and for a moment he appeared fascinated by what he had said.

Then he drew a breath, fixed his gaze on Will and said, 'I knew that Winchester would bring you running, son. Does it feel good?'

'You know it does,' Will said huskily.

'Fired her yet?'

'Not yet.'

'When you do,' Daniel Sagger said, 'you'll find her a sweeter gun than any you've handled.'

'That's fine, then,' Will said, wondering where all this was leading.

'I remember when your pa got that,' Cajun Pride said. 'Hell, I've never seen a finer shot—'

'Enough.' Daniel Sagger cut him short. He cast

another hard glance at Will, then reached over to slap Cajun Pride's horse and the two men moved away. They walked their horses up the slope, heading towards the crest beyond which the pale moon hung low and the skies were luminous.

'Get that Winchester out and ready,' Jake Cree said. 'They get to the top, take Cajun Pride with a single shot.'

'Jake, I can't do that!'

'You think your pa was talking for the sake of it?' Nelson said.

'You want me to back shoot him? A dying man?'

'If you don't,' Cree said, 'he's liable to back shoot your pa – because, sure as eggs is eggs, your pa ain't going to talk him round. The Utah Kid's responsible for your ma's death. Accessory to murder.'

'That's for the law to decide.'

'If you were listening,' Nelson said, 'you'll recall that your pa said something about talking to Pride's the least he can do for an old friend. But he put a maybe in there and, the way he acted, I think his mind was on a whole lot more.' He looked hard at Will. 'If it's in his mind, but he's in no position to act, then someone has to do it for him.'

'The man's got the cancer,' Jake Cree said softly. 'Wouldn't killing a man in that condition be an act of mercy?'

For a long moment, Will hesitated. Then he reached down and slid the shiny Winchester out of its boot. The stock was cold, the barrel icy. He slid his fingers through the lever, jacked a shell into the breech; looked up the slope.

The two men were approaching the crest, and it seemed to Will that, as they hit the top and became black outlines against the luminous skies, his pa moved away; placed a space as wide as a horse is long between him and Cajun Pride.

'How's your shoulder?' Cree said quickly. 'Will it hold steady for the shot, stand the strain?'

'It's fine.'

But what about me, Jake? Will thought. The battered shoulder will take it, the left arm will hold up for as long as it takes – but can I? Will I bear up under the strain of knowing what I've done? Live with that knowledge, day after day, for the rest of my life?

He licked his lips, lifted the rifle; again looked towards the ridge where the two mounted figures stood as if frozen.

All right, he thought, get on with it – for, when all's said and done, what wrong will I have committed? The man's in pain, dying. He killed my ma, and he'll kill my pa if I don't stop him.

Then, with a swift, decisive movement, he brought the Winchester '73 to his shoulder, drew a bead on Cajun Pride, and squeezed the trigger.

For all its speed, the action was slowed down in his mind, indelibly imprinted yet with the important details of what had happened, what did happen, confused and unclear. There was the crack of the shot; the sharp stab of pain in his left shoulder and the pause that seemed to stretch into eternity; the hiss of the bullet and the slow toppling of the man who went down as limp as a kid's rag doll. But for ever afterwards Will Sagger would look back and find himself wondering if, in that still and silent moment before he took the Utah Kid cleanly out of his saddle, the mortally sick man had turned his had slightly, seen what was about to happen – and deliberately remained motionless.

And if he really dug deep, Will would imagine that over that distant face seen in the half light of weak crescent moon he had seen the flickering of the faintest of smiles.

time but all plaster for his money will produce nothing strikdog in its basket will draw a growing relationship ...

... rose and held out his hands ...

"... you are considered, might have been called here."

"Just taking it through off."

"And who now—"

Pride looked it up, one shot out, his greying hair flopping over his forehead ...

"They're out there, whoever they are, you saw them – and Smithy knew it, and that's why you killed him."

"That was in your mind when you let me relieve him."

"Sure it was. But I figured it'd be maybe three men, not a posse, and I'd risk trailing them into the Hole ... come up against the men I've got, those other shootists at the cabin on the hill, distributing ..."

He lapsed into silence, squatting occasionally, ... the cigarette butts, ... pausing for some time and taking a draught of ... from the flask, huddled in his blanket and closing his eyes until the ...

Pride, who had sat in the light of sunset, watching the ... saddling up, tightening cinches ... towards the cabin – had digested what he ...

EPILOGUE

Harry Tracy was the mad dog of the Wild Bunch. Sullen, tight-lipped and with deep-set icy blue eyes, he was partnered by Dave Lant when the semi-illiterate killer, Swede Johnson, rode into Hole In The Wall in 1898. When Johnson killed seventeen-year-old Willy Strang over a minor incident, the three were forced to flee the Hole. Posses from three states hunted them down, and the outlaws were cornered near Powder Springs. There, Lant and Johnson surrendered, but Tracy fought on, dodging from rock to rock in a small canyon. Finally, in sub-zero temperatures, even Tracy was forced to surrender – on his terms! Three states – Utah, Colorado and Wyoming – fought over the three men. Lant and Tracy went to Colorado, Johnson to Wyoming, but Tracy proved far too slippery. Twice he broke out of the jail in Aspen and, although recaptured after the first break, on the second he made good his escape.

On 2 June, 1899, the first section of the Union Pacific's Overland Flyer was stopped at Wilcox,

Wyoming, by Robert Leroy Parker (Butch Cassidy), George Curry, Harvey Logan (Kid Curry) and Elza Lay. They used a red lantern placed on the track to stop the train, tried to force the engineer, W. R. (Rhinestone) Jones, to uncouple the express car and, when he refused, drove the train across a small wooden bridge. There, they blew the safe apart with dynamite – but, in a scene played out several times on modern-day television, they used too much explosive and sent $30,000 in bonds and banknotes fluttering into the air.

arguably spends bankered awkwardly, rolling yet another cigarette, gazing off into the gathering dusk, poking idly at the embers with a stick – exhibiting all the restless characterisms of men who had been too long idle yet were uncertain how to break away. And always, for each of them, there was the looming menace of the high purple cliffs set against the bleak western skies with the notch leading into Hole In The Wall cut into them like the sharp V of a rifle's rear sight.

Nothing had moved.

They had heard no sound.

'What I don't understand,' Dave Lee Nelson said, 'is why Daniel rode under that weird Cold Hand name, and how he kept that and his outlaw past under his hat for so long.'

Nelson, like Will earlier in the day, was riding away from the fire. He had ridden in on a lathered horse not too long after Daniel Sagger had headed back to the Hole, the badge on his vest glittering in the rays of the westering sun. Quickly, he'd set off saddle and brought the men up to date on the happenings back at Ten Mile – floating a spark of pride from time to time. It was told of his wife's part in the affair. Nelson mentioned his decision to ride into marshal with a war plan – as Dan Gillo – who nodded approval at the McCraes swift decision to send Nelson out to intercept the men chasing Daniel Sagger, em his already admired marshal's reputation soaring.

'Cold Hand,' Gillo said, in answer to his question, 'because there never was a man could hold a six-shooter steadier than Daniel. Hand, keep it under another. Well, I guess he lost himself in the world of mustang-ranching, and when he did that he lost everybody else, too.'

'Until Captis Tillet got sick and ambitious and decided to hunt him down,' Jake Cree said bitterly.

For a few moments there was silence as all four of them reflected on what was, and what might have been. Then Cree said, 'You were about to say, Slim.'

'If they'll stop the train tonight, I've said that and I'm sure of it,' Slim Cillit said at last. His points crackling like distant gunfire as he eased closer to the fire. 'That deadline means they're already short of time, they'll be looking at somewhere real close. So, sticking my neck out, I say they'll hit the Overland Flyer about ten miles after it pulls out of Casper.'

'And stopping it's their first problem,' Jake said, eyes narrowed to thought. 'You reckon what, Slim? A barrier of some kind, a pile of rocks or timber?'

'Lantern,' the deputy said. 'Faster and easier to wave their down with a red light. Ain't a train driver around who'll not at least slow down out of curiosity – and when he does that, they've got him.'

Will sat listening to the two older men, Will Sugges boy, rigidly moving his shoulder to prevent it softening while finding it difficult to reconcile that often he knew of old with this now man who was... it paint with a band of outlaws. And despite knowing he'd be dragged into it, despite his pa's reassurance that it would be over quickly, Will couldn't rid his mind of the awful conviction that those words had been for his benefit and had hidden Daniel Sugges deep uncertainty and misgiving.